From The Women's
34 Great Sutton Stree

Yvonne du Fresne was born in 1929 and was brought up in the Danish-French Huguenot community of the Manawatu in New Zealand. She has had a full-time teaching career and now lives in retirement on Makara Beach, Wellington.

She has published four books: *Farvel and Other Stories* (1982), *The Book of Ester* (1982), and *The Growing of Astrid Westergaard and Other Stories* (1985) and *Frédérique* (1987).

Praise for *Farvel and Other Stories*:

'Her stories race with vitality and immediacy... *Farvel* speaks across all cultures' *Aukland Star*

'Du Fresne's wit and her control of pace and tone are admirably assured' *New Zealand Listener*

'A delightful gem of a book, beautiful, evocative, nostalgia-invoking and written in a "readable" but masterly style' *The Star*, Christchurch

Yvonne du Fresne

The Bear from the North

Tales of a New Zealand Childhood

The Women's Press

First published by the Women's Press Limited 1989
A member of the Namara Group
34 Great Sutton Street, London EC1V 0DX

Copyright © Yvonne du Fresne 1989

All rights reserved. This is a work of fiction
and any resemblance to persons living or dead is purely coincidental

British Library Cataloguing in Publication Data
Du Fresne, Yvonne, 1929–
 The bear from the north: tales of a
 New Zealand childhood
 I. Title
 823 [F]

ISBN 0-7043-4187-5

The following stories were first published in *Farvel and Other Stories*, Victoria University Press, Wellington, 1980: 'The Spy', 'The School', 'The System', 'The Looters', 'Arts and Crafts', 'The Mound', 'My Bedstemoder', 'Arbor Day', 'The Garden Party', 'The School Picnic', 'The Old Ones', 'Armistice Day', 'Centennial Exhibition', 'Astrid of the Limberlost' and 'Farvel'. The remaining stories appeared in *The Growing of Astrid Westergaard and Other Stories*, Longman Paul, Auckland, 1985, although an earlier version of 'Guy Fox' was first published in *All the Dangerous Animals are in Zoos* (Longman Paul, New Zealand, 1981) and 'The Growing of Astrid Westergaard' was first published in *The Summer Book* (Port Nicholson Press, New Zealand, 1982).

Typset by AKM Associates
Ajmal House, Hayes Road, Southall, Greater London
Printed and bound in Great Britain by
Cox & Wyman, Reading, Berks

Contents

Introduction   vii
The Spy   1
The School   7
The System   15
The Looters   20
Arts and Crafts   26
Houses   31
Guy Fox   38
Gods and Heroes   42
The Mound   48
My Bedstemoder   52
Arbor Day   58
The Garden Party   63
The Followers   69
The Swans   77
The School Picnic   82
The Old Ones   87
Armistice Day   92
Coronation Day   98
Centennial Exhibition   104
The Woman from Norway   109
The Battle Charge   114
The Young Kings   119
Astrid of the Limberlost   125
The Headmaster   132
The Cousin from Holstein   138
The Growing of Astrid Westergaard   144
Farvel   151

Introduction

My family formed part of a group of Danes, who left their ancestral lands in South Jutland in 1876, after experiencing the first period of the Prussian Occupation which followed Denmark's defeat in the Slesvig-Holstein War of 1864. The occupation was designed to make their region part of a 'greater Germany', with suppression of their language and culture, compulsory military service for young Danes in the German Army and very little economic help for farming. These people, whose family histories in their districts reached back before church records began, had endured previous enemy occupations and clung to their culture with such tenacity that they earned themselves the nickname of 'Super-Danes' from their fellow countrymen! These enforced 'absences' from the mainstream of Danish life, however, helped to preserve their very old Danish culture, rich in custom, folklore and beliefs, which they carried with them to New Zealand.

Links between New Zealand and Scandinavia stretch back to the arrival of the first Europeans in 1642: the crew of the *Heemskerck* and the *Zeehaen*, the ships of the Dutch navigator Abel Tasman, included some Scandinavians, and Captain Cook had Solander, a Swedish botanist, on his first voyage in 1769.

Scandinavians do not seem to have been amongst the first settlers, but during the 1860s a few arrived. The most outstanding was Bishop Monrad, the ex-premier of Denmark, who left his country with his wife and family after the Slesvig-Holstein War and took up land in the Manawatu. From 1870 to 1875 the New

A Bear From the North

Zealand Government turned to the northern countries of Europe for migrants, and by 1878 there were 4,600 Scandinavians in the colony, about half of them Danes.

In February 1871, fifty-one Norwegian settlers from the ship *Celaeno* arrived at Foxton, the port of the Manawatu, followed in March by a party of seventy-six Scandinavians (including fifty-six Danes) from the ship *England*. With such a comparatively large foreign-speaking population, the township of Palmerston North in its early years had rather an exotic flavour.

H.W.F. Halcombe, Immigration Agent for the general government, reported: 'On their first arrival, there was a great popular prejudice amounting to indignation against them, but this feeling has been changed by the example of their steady, persevering industry into one of entire approbation.'

Twelve months after the arrival of the first batch of immigrants, the *Wellington Independent* reported that 'Up till this time the poor fellows had considerable difficulties to contend with . . . but I am happy to be able to state that most of them are now beginning to make themselves very comfortable upon the land allotted them, many of them surprisingly so, considering the up-hill nature of the task. Anyone acquainted with obstacles to settlement in this part of the province, the heavy rich bottom land, the densely timbered forest, must admit that to have done so well in the time is no slight praise to the perseverance and high qualities as settlers displayed by these people . . .'

The Scandinavian settlement in the Manawatu was large enough to remain distinct. Its settlers kept up their language and culture, with its long roots in myth, symbolism and history, its practicality and rich tradition of the importance of home and family, equality, cooperative work-habits, child-rearing and care of the aged: a life-giving source for settlement in a new country.

Faced with the appalling 'heavy rich bottom land' as the *Wellington Independent* so tactfully described those mosquito-ridden wastelands allocated to them, the Danish settlers applied their traditional farming skills learned in the original 'sand-and-water' of their part of Jutland, and slowly established rich farmland. Success in farming and business ventures in Palmerston North

Introduction

meant that the families kept up their links with Denmark, which still continue.

The first Lutheran church service was held, in Danish, in Palmerston North in 1872, and a Lutheran church was built in 1882. Services in Danish were held until 1929, when English was introduced. The church has continued and prospered with the addition over the years of more northern European settlers, and in 1987 it was rebuilt on a much larger scale.

A small number of settlers from the French-Huguenot colony in Fredericia, Denmark, followed my grandfather, Abraham du Fresne, after he settled in Palmerston North in 1890.

The young adults of my family who arrived in 1877 married within the Scandinavian settlement, and half of the first generation intermarried. Those of us in the second generation mostly married 'outside' New Zealanders and new European settlers. We are still a warm, lively, extended family, aware of our old culture, vigorously participating in the life of New Zealand, and keeping constant links with our families in Denmark. In 1987 we celebrated our heritage with the third generation at our *enormous* family reunion.

Yvonne du Fresne
Wellington, 1988

The Bear from the North

The Spy

How can I tell you of those great plains where I began? It is so early in the morning when I first saw the world.

Somebody puts me down on the ground. Somebody pushes my hands down. My fingers feel warm, hard earth. My fingers touch thick jointed grass. The grass will not keep still. It glitters, it moves under my hands like a living animal. I climb to my feet and stagger. The animal I have touched is moving away from me. Under the great soup-bowl of the sky the animal runs – the grass runs. The world is grass thrashing to the sky's rim. The gale roars, the sky booms, the grass boils.

A voice over my head laughs. It calls out in Danish to my Fader, then it speaks to me in English.

'Feel thy land!' says the voice, dark as chocolate snapping. 'Feel thy *land*.'

I drop to my haunches, I clumsily pull a stalk of the long grass from the summer ground. I put it in my mouth and chew. My mouth tastes of gales, of artesian water, of sun. My mouth tastes the Manawatu for the first time in my life.

Ah, but soon I walked. Soon I lifted my eyes from my feet and started watching. I watched and listened for the rest of my life. Astrid the spy.

In the farm-house of the Danish settlers of the Manawatu there was light everywhere. The land and the sky came through the windows. The long muslin curtains moved in and out, in and out, moving to the heartbeat of the plains, of that grass that slept sometimes, and leapt to its feet when the gales started, and ran to the edge of the earth.

But inside our rooms the light from the sky washed everything in white. Aunts, cousins, my Moder, my Bedstemoder sat gossiping over their embroidery, over the blue and white coffee cups, in the long afternoons. Their faces swam, melted in light. Where were we? New Zealand? Or Jutland? The voices ran on in the deep, gutteral Danish. Those women could change anything. They were magic women. The Norner. One moment we were in summer in the Manawatu. The next moment we were in the floating, mysterious white days and nights of midsummer in Denmark. Houses, trees, people swayed and dissolved, became something else. The Jutland spy, Astrid Westergaard, watched the land through slit eyes, trying to find New Zealand.

In the room of Tante Helga, my kindergarten teacher, I touched everything I saw, I ran my fingers over wooden toys. The voice of my Tante Helga could make me do anything. I stumbled around dancing. I sang a Danish song about a Nisse. My hands ran over and over the wooden doll she gave me to feel, to help me learn the world. Its eyes stared into mine. Its painted mouth smiled. It had a peasant scarf painted on its black hair. It was a Russian lady. I looked at the smile painted on her wooden face. 'Where do you come from?' I asked her.

'Russia,' she said. 'Where do you come from?'

'I do not know my country yet,' I said, 'But I am going to find it. I am Astrid the spy,' I said. 'I watch. I listen. My Bedstemoder says that my blood was formed in the Jutland marshes. And now here we are in New Zealand. I was born here. I am a New Zealand girl. And now I mean to find New Zealand,' I said.

So I set out on my life-journey of observation. To make my discoveries. To find New Zealand.

I penetrated my first English house; the house of Hilary Pennyfeather, that descendant of the British Empire. For we lived in New Zealand, a country that was coloured rose-pink, and an ancient country of the British Empire. But the houses of the Empire were not bathed in white or pink light. They were steeped in the noble gloom of old battles, forced marches, mud, and heroes and their horses dying with rolling eyes under Union Jacks, torn to ribbons by the roaring cannon.

Once inside Hilary Pennyfeather's house, I never once blinked, in case I missed the smallest sign.

For here was a house of the military, of the descendants of those who had died for the Empire. Some of their older wars were preserved in pictures in back bedrooms. All the rooms in Hilary Pennyfeather's farmhouse were shaded by blinds and thick lace curtains, in honour of the dead, the glory of the Empire. I screwed up my eyes all the better to see the pictures. Soldiers, waving swords and shouting. Horses writhing, but resigned to their noble death.

Modern wars were commemorated in ingenious ways. A brooch on Hilary's mother's bosom, of two clasped hands, with the mysterious word 'Mizpah' welded on to them. Blurred brown photographs of peaked tents and carefree lounging soldiers. Paintings of those soldiers, their lounging days left far behind, crawling up cliffs with neat puffs of cannon fire around them, and rows of dark evil faces intent over rifles peering from the ramparts above. And on a sad tea caddy, brown with age and cannon smoke, a doomed cavalry regiment endlessly charging around it.

I sat up at the table, cheerfully waiting for the afternoon tea to come, for the usual gay voices talking of this and of that, me with them. I should have known better, I should have not been such a fool.

'Come along, Aster,' said Hilary's Moder in the brisk brief voice of the ladies of the British Empire, 'little girls have their afternoon tea break in the playroom. Come along now. Go with Hilary. Chop-chop!' Chop-chop . . . Quick as Thor's magic axe she must know about, I slid off the chair, sucked in my stomach, and walked lightly and quickly after Hilary. Girls of the Empire, going to tea in the playroom. It was a lesson in the spartan qualities of the Empire. I made my spine a ramrod of steel, I rehearsed in my mind my new light, cool voice. I wanted to learn how to endure hunger, cold, forced marches, and perhaps, a cavalry charge. I prayed that I might choke on one of the afternoon tea cakes, and be brought back from the dead by a smart thump on my back by Hilary, and recover, and say 'Don't worry – it was nothing.' For that was what

The Bear from the North

Hilary and her friends said when they were thrown by their Shetland ponies.

It was not to be. I gazed at the tray brought in by Hilary into the playroom, a bleak empty room, with a tiled fireplace where the wind moaned in the chimney, remembering the Crimean War and Waterloo. The walls were varnished brown. The floorboards were varnished brown. I gazed at the tray as Hilary, who was athletic, smartly banged the door shut with one foot. On a plate lay thin slices of white bread, with here and there a wan speck of colour.

'Hundreds and thousands,' said Hilary, gloating over the specks. '*Fairy* bread.'

But the milk jug was the worst. It had a painting of a street with a ragged child in it. He had a coat hanging to his ragged boots, and a crushed top-hat. He was grinning. I knew where he lived. In that soot-blackened foreign city – London. He spent his days crawling up chimneys, cleaning them. His master lit fires in the hearth beneath his feet, to make him work faster.

Inside the jug lay the milk. It was blue with little patches of skin on it. Nobody's teeth could grow strong from that milk. If I drank that milk, I would get tuberculosis and my teeth would fall out.

I was sick on the varnished floorboards. And when it was over, Hilary said 'Bad *luck*,' and I sat and bawled for my Moder, and forgot how to be a spartan girl of the British Empire.

When I was safe home again, Fader tried to cheer me up.

'Ah,' he said, 'just wait until you are a true school girl.'

'A school girl?'

'In one month,' he said, 'you will be a proper school girl. Marching about, and so on.'

'How can I be a true school girl if I am sick on people's floors?' I roared.

'Hah!' cried Far. 'Now listen, and do not be like your Onkel Henning. Now he thought he knew all about New Zealand schools. Not a word of English did we have. There we were in our lille Dunskie caps . . .'

'With the embroidery!' sang my Bedstemoder tenderly.

'With the embroidery,' said my Fader grimly. 'Helga, Henning and me. We said we'd stick together at playtime. Nobody could understand us anyway. But that old Henning now – he had heard of the British Public School from some fool who should have known better. The fool said to Henning – these schools here are the same as the English Public Schools. At playtime, they fight you. The whole school. You have to prove your brave heart.

'So Henning prepared, out in the stables. Dancing on his toes, hitting the air, hissing through his teeth and so on. Working out his battle cry – an old Danish one. On the first day it was hell. We didn't understand a word. We kept our mouths shut. But not Henning. At playtime, Helga and me, in a corner by a fence, looked up, and there was Henning . . .'

'So sweet in his lille cap,' crooned my Bedstemoder.

'. . . looking like a bersaerk – fists up, dancing on his toes, and yelling his old Norse battle cry at one hundred and fifty English, who steadily marched upon him.'

'He fought,' intoned my Bedstemoder, 'like the true Viking of old.'

'He was carried home,' said my Fader, 'with both eyes closed.'

There was a short silence. My Mor looked dreamily at the road running past our farm. A Ford motorcar raised a slow dust cloud in the distance. She pointed at the dust cloud.

'All up that road,' she said nostalgically, 'I ran. With my lille headscarf on. And the embroidered apron back-to-front.'

'Mmm,' sang my Bedstemoder, patting my Moder's lap to comfort her.

'I ran *so* fast,' said my Moder, 'that none could catch me. I fell under the wire fence. My Fader saw me. He yelled over the field "Defy them!" Not a word of English we had.'

'What a good Christian man he was,' said Bedstemoder.

'So I defied them. In Danish.'

'Ha!' hooted my Far, restlessly pacing to the window and peering at the vanishing Ford car. 'Such courage!'

'I became the fastest runner at the school sports for evermore.'

'Ja,' said my Bedstemoder, 'such limbs! I remember.'

I looked at the distant school over the paddocks, rearing its red brick splendour out of its mournful clump of bush, full of the Grenadier Guards and warriors from the Maori Wars. My mouth gaped in its shameful crying shape.

'Now, now,' said Far rapidly, to avert the first roar. 'Limbs like your Moder you have. Who is the fastest runner in the Manawatu?'

'Me,' I roared, 'me!'

The School

At the age of six, I stood in the middle of the Manawatu Plains. The grass rippled past me to the sky's edge. It sighed in my ears –

'Astr-id, Astr-id . . .'

I looked the Plains in the eye.

'I know you,' I said. 'I know you by heart. And I know myself,' I said.

I looked at my world.

The vegetable garden, the flower garden, and the canal that my Fader had made. Three ducks rode its ripples – up – down, up – down. Our white wooden house. The stone paved yard on which my Moder flung buckets of water. First smoking hot – then hissing cold. Inside the house, in vases, were the living symbols of the Plains – the seed heads of fennel, the bunches of Plains-grass, the blades of young flax, flowers from the garden. On the wall, pictures of embroidered grass bearing its seed, the clouds, the water, the birds hanging in the sky.

I knew those signs of the land by heart. I was in training to be a Norne – the fate-teller of my people. I noted down in my head each morning the patterns of the clouds, of the birds; the patterns of men's lives. Inside my house, I scrabbled my fingers through the fat wooden beads in Tante Helga's bead box. Squinting with concentration, I threaded them along scarlet cords. I loaded my neck with Norne's necklaces, Dronning's necklaces. I climbed on to my cushion in the living room, and sat, like a great Dronning in her horned building, waiting to hear my history from my Wise Men.

The Bear from the North

I looked at the Russian doll clutched in my hands. Her dress and her headscarf were decorated with pink and purple roses, orange tulips, and scarlet hearts. She was a doll who had lived in the countries of the north. The designs on her dress were constant reminders of the lands we had left – the life going on in the tall dark houses of Denmark. Coffee being drunk out of the blue and white porcelain cups, the snow falling, the church bells ringing, and the skeins of swan and wild geese slowly unwinding into their arrow-shape for long travel from Denmark, for flight to strange lands. And here we were, at the end of our flight. The Russian doll was shaped like a good strong onion, built for survival in new lands.

'Now you will hear your true history,' she said to me as we both sat on our cushions, waiting for the Wise Men to begin.

The Wise Men were my Grandonkels. They sat in giants' armchairs, filling their pipes. This was their preparation for the history-telling. They smelt of explosives from their wax-vesta matches igniting the tobacco in their immense Danish pipes. They smelled of their volcano-hot coffee made from acorns that they ground and red-hot coffee beans sent out from Denmark, laced with snaps and smoking hot cream.

They instructed me in the true history of the small northern nations of Europe, where we had survived blizzards, bears, the Northern Lights, ice and reindeers.

The voices of the Grandonkels boiled and wheezed in huskiness and glottal stops.

'Now in Denmark in Olden Times,' cried Onkel Sigurd, 'there was a great queen – Dronning Margrethe! She united Denmark with Norway. They faced the Swedes. The Swedish hordes charged across the ice. Dronning Margrethe sat on her horse and faced them. She knew the ice!'

'Ha!' wheezed the other old voices. '*She* knew – *she* knew!'

'The Swedes sank forlorn into their watery graves,' continued Onkel Sigurd, voice cracking like the treacherous ice. 'Oh – that was a great day for Denmark!'

'Great times ... Denmark ...' sang the other old voices, and fell silent in clouds of tobacco smoke.

I sat on my throne and put myself into my history. The winter winds howled across northern Europe. I rode my horse, with my dronning-crown of silver set on my head. I raised one arm to my people. In the other I held the Dannebrog. Denmark's flag. It rippled its scarlet and white folds against the walls of ice invading Denmark from the Arctic.

'Ho!' I cried. 'The ice is coming! Dansk folk, throw back the ice!'

All day long we fought. When darkness fell our victory was complete.

We had defeated Winter.

But over the paddocks from its brooding patch of bush, the school sent out its dark chants faintly on the wind. Cocking my ear, I heard it come and go –

> 'Twice two are four!
> Twice three are six!'

The day came to go to school. I blew out the candles on my birthday cake, decorated with pink sugar hearts and paper Dannebrogs to give me heart. The next morning dawned. I clutched my Moder's hand. We stood at the school gate. My Moder was dressed in her tweed three-piece costume and the hat over one eye to give *her* heart. The farm land ran up to the school fence and stopped. Over the fence it changed to school land, stained with ink, that vanished into dark brooding trees. The trees rose seriously up into the sky.

'Remember and record accurately,' said the trees.

The school was of pink brick with two noble marble panels surrounded by a stern concrete framework. The panels were empty – waiting for the first names in gold letters to go up. Achievements of sport and learning. With dates. On the school roof rose up tin chimneys, a little open to admit fresh air for learning facts. As much air as was needed, and no more.

My Mor clutched me, and swallowed.

'Farvel, lille Astrid,' she said to me, as one who is farewelling a soldier off to the cruel wars.

But there was no speech from me. I wore my blue linen tunic with the blouse underneath embroidered in magic signs. Wheat-ears, cornflowers, and some dronning-crowns. They were to save me from peril.

'Come – come!' cried a voice. 'Put your shoulders back, Astrid!'

I looked up. A woman as thin as leather stood on some steps. She was wearing a knitted two-piece. She wore a blouse and a man's tie. She wore men's shoes.

'Poor soul,' murmured my Moder in Danish, 'no man's-love has she known.'

Then my Moder was gone – walking home alone in the three-piece costume and the hat over one eye for the admiration of the wild flowers in the grass beside the road.

'You may call me Miss Gore,' said the leather teacher in quite a different voice.

'I am Astrid Frederikke Dagmar Westergaard,' I said. 'Goddag.'

'Dear me,' said Miss Gore, looking seriously at another teacher dressed in a brown blouse, and a blue knitted two-piece. 'Dear me!'

'Goddag,' I said to this new one. She did not respond. They bent over a long thin book. Miss Gore wrote in it very lightly indeed with a pencil. They both drew back and shook their heads.

'Right across this column,' said Miss Gore. 'How am I to fit it in with all those *letters*?'

'How indeed?' said the brown teacher. They looked at the long thin book. Miss Gore sucked her pencil and gave a tiny shrug.

'I will abbreviate,' said Miss Gore. 'There is a little ostentation here, I think.'

'Oh, quite!' said the other.

Quait. I closed my eyes to savour the sound. When I opened them I was being pulled through a door into a high room. Hundreds of children drooped over iron desks. A lady with pink eyes struck a board with a long stick.

'And?' she cried.

'Four!' roared hundreds of voices. She struck the board again.

'Think!' she cried.

Oh – they *thought*. They lay their arms and heads down on the iron desks and screwed their eyes shut. Then they supported one arm with the other, waved them and groaned. They snapped the fingers of their waving arms, bodies bent over. The air was full of whip cracks. Teeth were bared.

'Yes?' asked the lady.

'Six!' shouted a hoarse voice. Ah – how they groaned with grim laughter, how they snapped their whip-cracking fingers.

I was pushed down into my iron desk. The sides touched my legs with frost. I ran my fingers over the iron. A hand pulled my shoulders up.

'Sit up straight,' said Miss Gore, transformed into a great field marshal. She stood on the toes of her man's shoes, her nostrils flared and scented ink, chalk, old wood, mud and blood. The Grenadier Guards, the Maori warriors crouched under the window-sill outside.

'Think – think – think!' rapped out Miss Gore.

'Eight!' roared a voice.

'Thank *you*!' said the pink-eyed lady, as crisply as a snapping stick of chalk, and smartly wrote '8' on the board. The arms dropped back, their owners popped fingers into their mouths, and sucked wide-eyed at Miss Gore.

'Now!' cried Miss Gore, with devilish anticipation, 'Who-am-I-going-to-choose-today?'

'Me-me-me!' moaned the voices again. Each child flung a beseeching hand up, supported with immense pain by the other arm. Eyes screwed tight, teeth snarled.

Miss Gore darted her finger out – once, twice.

'Avis! And – May!'

Two sturdy girls stood up, hanging their heads with meek pride under giant hair bows. Miss Gore pulled a string that vanished into her bosom. She busily hauled and out popped a watch! She consulted it with a frown, working out long-division and decimal sums in her head.

'Eleven-thirty!' she cried. 'Off you go!' They bundled out of the door, hair ribbons bobbing. 'Let us not pause!' cried Miss Gore, 'One, two three, four, five!'

Heads ducked, desk lids flew back with a crash, shoulders stooped like old men, desk lids shut like bullets exploding, books slammed open, arms went behind heads. I slowly opened my desk. Inside was nothing but an ink stain, a sad smell, and a piece of crumpled paper. I lifted it out and lowered the desk. I shakily smoothed out my paper, my school work. A contorted face drawn in red ink met mine. The face was Miss Gore's. I started to raise it, to show Miss Gore her portrait. A hand reached over my desk. The paper vanished. A girl in an orange and black checked dress and a buster-cut stared straight ahead. She busily sucked a pencil, very bitten at the end. She frowned at the front of the room. The lady with the pink eyes was drawing so softly with red chalk on the blackboard. She sucked in her lips, she held her breath. Very faintly she drew a little round shape and worried it a little. She changed to green chalk. I watched with rapture. I seized the buster-cut girl's arm.

'Aeble!' I said in my deep dronning's voice. 'Apple!' It rang in the room.

'Sh-sh Westergaard!' rapped Miss Gore's voice. I craned around to see who was this Westergaard. There was nobody I could see. The buster-cut girl wrote, frowned, groaned, licked her finger and rubbed a little hole in her paper. She covered her little hole with a hand. I watched the lovely little hole she had made like the fox. Miss Gore paced up and down, a very keen-eyed field marshal. I pointed to the hole. 'There is a hole she has made!' I cried in Danish. 'She has made a neat little hole!'

'Sh-sh, Westergaard!' snapped Miss Gore. I looked up again to see this Westergaard. Then I saw the photographs. I gazed and gazed. Dronninger, konger, laden with furs, hair, crowns, crosses and rows of diamonds and pearls gazed down on me. English konger. Frowning. I was in the heart of the British Empire. The kings and queens gazed steely-eyed at me, dressed in their dragon-robes of royalty, holding the treasure brought to them from the British Empire.

The door jerked open. Two scarlet faces under hair ribbons appeared.

'We came back quick!' gasped the first hair-ribbon. The second hair-ribbon heaved something through the door.

'It were heavy but we were good quick girlies for you, Miss Gore!'

'Splendid – splendid!' cried Miss Gore, striding down the aisle. The two hair-ribbons bobbed over the floor to the table, bearing a great brown wooden tray. On it lay plates covered with other plates.

'*Time*, I think, Miss Prendergast!' cried Miss Gore, hauling out the rope from within her bosom. 'What is twelve o'clock?' asked Miss Gore skittishly.

The School

'*Lunch* time!' roared the hundreds.

'Lunch time!' agreed Miss Gore, popping the watch back. 'Listen!' She raised a finger like the prophet of old.

Faintly in the immense dark school roof a bell rang for the dead. The class folded its arms over bulging chests, sat up like cossacks and frowned fiercely.

'Stand,' said Miss Gore graciously. With a roar like the ocean they stood, stepped out in the aisle and clenched their hands into fists at their sides.

'For-ward!' sang Miss Gore.

Line after line marched out. Through the door came the sound of the bell tolling for the dead, men shouting, and somebody screaming. The girl with the buster-cut glanced at me.

'You need a pencil,' she said.

'Ja!'

'You need a pencil,' she said, 'At school you write with pencils.' Then she folded her lips into a tight line, climbed into the aisle, changed into a pouter-pigeon, and marched out tippy-toes.

I stayed in the silence with the British Rulers. Not a mouse stirred. The two hair-ribbons were standing with bowed heads by a cupboard. Miss Gore opened it and whipped out a sad brown tin. She rummaged about with her fingertips and extracted two brown lumps.

'Open wide,' said Miss Gore. They opened wide their beaks as Miss Gore popped the two lumps in. 'Off you go!' said Miss Gore. 'You can take the tray back to my sister's afterwards.' She rapidly unwound a napkin from a silver ring. The two hair-ribbons chewed, choked, clapped hands to mouths and ran from the room, exploding with pride.

Miss Gore laid the napkin with care on to her meagre lap, and lifted a pudding plate off a dinner plate. There lay a sad brown dinner, faintly steaming. Miss Gore delicately cut at a heap of silverbeet and raised a forkful. Then she looked up, and froze.

'I am *eating*, Westergaard,' said a voice as terrible as the end of the world. 'Little girls do not *watch* people *eating*!'

'Nej! Nej!' I agreed huskily, crashing out of the iron desk. I picked up my new bag. I passed the board and looked up at the aeble. There it hung in red chalk, with its little leaf and stem.

The Bear from the North

'Aeble,' I said cheerfully. 'You got your aeble there, I see.'

Miss Gore's cheeks moved like the rabbit's when it ate its grass.

'Out!' she mumbled through the silverbeet.

'Oh, ja,' I agreed amicably.

I fell into the open air. Buster Cut waved a friendly hand from a damp seat on a mud bank.

'Goddag,' I said, dumping down my school-bag. I opened it. There lay the miracle – a peanut-butter jar with something red and creamy flashing at me. Beside it lay a little silver spoon. Dumbfounded I opened the jar. Fruit jelly with cream winked up at me.

'Rødgrød,' I growled at Buster Cut, 'good *food*'. I started in with the silver spoon, then stooped and stared. In the mud lay a little carefully formed hollow. In the hollow lay a clutch of glass balls, each as round as the aeble on the blackboard inside that other place.

I pointed with my mouth full.

'Marbles,' said Buster Cut, as if to the unlettered savage.

'Nej,' I said, '*aeg*.' I pulled my words together for her sake. 'Eggs,' I said, 'lille eggs in nest.' Clutching the peanut-butter jar I levered myself down and touched them. 'Lille eggs in nest,' I said. 'Lille *eggs*!'

The System

The sun rose in scarlet. The Plains shouted to see the flames in the sky. I crouched over my bowl and speared the first mushroom. Somebody had brought in the flavour of the Plains – the summer-dried grass flashing its spears under the thick autumn dews, browned sticks of thistles still holding the ferocity of the sun sending needles of shock into my bare legs, the cold wet grass soothing them. Who was the sorceress? I looked up. There she was. My Bedstemoder lightly touched the mushrooms as she leant over the seething pan. She turned and looked at me.

'Mush-r-room!' she said.

'Ja!' I said.

Then she looked at Tante Helga.

'You not having my mush-r-room?' she asked, bland as milk. Tante Helga haughtily continued squeezing the bitter lemon juice that ran down her long pale fingers on to the soaked raisins and sultanas that made up her fearful, healthy breakfasts.

'You know my rules of diet,' said Tante Helga richly. '*Never* a cold!'

She gave the mushrooms a bleak look. And no wonder. For who had picked them?

Tante Helga.

And where had she picked them?

In the Lessingtons' cow paddock. For who had gone off in search of Nature's healthy exercise for the body and God's beautiful wild pathways over strange farmers' paddocks?

Tante Helga.

The Bear from the North

Athletically vaulting over the Lessington fence she had gone after mushrooms as big as dinner plates. There had been a little fracas. Fader, alternately hooting with laughter and shouting with rage, had had to go and rescue her.

'What did Mr Lessington do to Tante Helga?' I asked Bedstemoder as she sat peeling the mushrooms with her fingers.

'He locked her in his wash-house,' said Bedstemoder serenely, picking up a very large mushroom indeed, and admiring it. But now Tante Helga was changing her character again.

In front of our eyes she was turning from the wild free child of God into the responsible Kindergarten teacher, heavy with the responsibility of educating the nation.

We ran through the little points again.

'Have you threaded the beads to learn the colours?'

'Ja!'

'Have you formed the letters and patterns in the sand tray?'

'Ja!'

'Have you formed the modelling wax into this and that?'

'Oh, ja. Little nests and snakes. My nests are judged to be good!'

'So,' said Tante Helga heavily, squinting as the full charge of the lemon juice hit her stomach. She took in a sharp breath then stirred the raisins and sultanas about with one finger. Tante Helga followed the teachings of Madame Montessori for the education of the young, and *Health and Beauty* magazines for the health of the body.

'You will wither away,' said my Bedstemoder, casting but one glance at Tante Helga's bowl of acid.

I bent over the last of my mushrooms. I needed their strength, their magic. For you must know; I lied. I lied every morning. There were no sand trays. I had never reached the reward of the bead-threading. And the modelling wax was plasticine, coloured grey and smelling of little children's tears. I had never touched it. The others did – the clever ones who had beaten the System.

The System was Arithmetic first. You had to get it all correct. Then you did the Spelling, the Printing, the Reading, the Writing of Stories. Then, at two o'clock you lolled back like a lord in your iron desk and modelled the snakes, the little nests, from the plasticine. The clever ones indolently rolled the little balls of

The System

plasticine, preparatory to making the nests, the snakes, and looked at Edna Woods, Chrissy Hamilton – and me. There we sat at two o'clock, gripping our bitten pencils, still doing the Arithmetic. But I was struggling to defeat that System.

Each morning I rose, did Tante Helga's deep breathing, facing the rising sun, and gulped in its red flames for strength. Then I ate a giant's breakfast and set off to school chanting my runes. Or Miss Gore's runes. She used them as she passed out the Arithmetic Papers each morning.

'One, two, three, four, five!' chanted Miss Gore, dispensing papers as the God Thor gave out his thunder bolts to his warriors in the sky. 'Head up, shoulders back, use your handkerchief!' chanted Miss Gore. I added those words too. I crossed my fingers, looked the clouds in the eye and said each morning, 'Freyja, give me wisdom. Thor give me strength.' I added for extra protection, 'Gentle Jesus, meek and mild, *make me know those hard sums!*'

Nobody listened.

Each morning I gripped my pencil and waited. Miss Gore turned the blackboard round. There were her written runes. And each morning I wrote her more and more powerful runes. I hid my paper behind one fiercely cupped hand and drew my first dots. Then I traced a magic line to join them up. As Astrid the spy, I learned the other children's movements off by heart. They bent over their papers, sighed, chewed their pencils, wrote busily, and rubbed out with one wet finger. Oh, I did all that! I followed my pencil's pattern. It was following the whispered commands of the Goddess Freyja. High above the school she hovered in her cloak of falcon feathers, learning all men's secrets, guiding my pencil in the most powerful runes in the world. When I had finished, I put down my pencil, stood up and smoothed my skirt to guard against an ancient spell called The Poppy Show, and marched up to join the serpent. The serpent was the line of clever children who waited to reach Miss Gore's table, which was decked out like an altar with a paperweight, a tray of pencils and a serious-looking green vase holding one flower and two leaves. The children standing in the serpent scratched an arm or a leg, tossed back their hair and frowned at the ceiling. I did none of those things. I stood bowed like an old Jutland peasant, waiting to get to the priest's altar for

The Bear from the North

my sign from God. When I laid my paper softly before Miss Gore, it was always the same. She raised her eyebrows, turned down the corners of her mouth, and placed a small pink kiss in the bottom right-hand corner. I never had a nice soft voice for Miss Gore in that room. I had my Bedstemoder's voice – as deep as doom. 'You like my *work*?' I boomed at Miss Gore each day. Miss Gore always drew in her breath and looked thinner when she heard that voice.

'Avis,' said Miss Gore. 'Avis – show the Westergaard child how to do the Story of Five, will you dear? Again?'

I looked up to find this Westergaard for the hundredth time. But I knew him. Oh yes. He tripped over desks, chewed pencils to splinters, had a voice like the end of the world, and was never privileged to carry the dinner tray for Miss Gore.

Avis advanced with her special, rueful smile for Miss Gore. Miss Gore gave the same smile back. Summoning up strength to deal with that Westergaard. And you know who that Westergaard was? It was me. My other self that grew up in that school. Westergaard the bear from the North. Westergaard whose families ate raw fish in the winter. At home I moved like a little feather, my Moder said, but in that school, I had feet like stone and a head like a rock.

That day, Avis pushed Westergaard the bear into its desk and sat down. She flicked back her hair and ran her pencil down a new piece of paper. The pencil was as sharp as a needle. The signs Avis made were needle marks, as thin as frost-splinters.

'Tak,' said Westergaard, in a voice like a bull. At that word 'tak' Avis turned an offended pink to be reminded that she was sitting beside one of those people who ate raw fish in the winter. She went back to her desk and neatly turned upside down to get a book from the tidy pile within.

'Kom!' said a voice as cold, as dark as marsh-water. *Our* voice. I twisted my head. 'Kom,' said a girl with two plaits behind me. Her plaits were as white as buttermilk. She moved like lightning on to the end of my seat.

'Goddag lille Astrid,' she said.

'Goddag!' I boomed.

'Sh-sh! said Anna Friis, pushing my head down. 'Look at this wonderful Story of Five, you youp.'

The System

I looked.

'Give me your five fingers.'

'Oh ja,' I said happily, copying her deep voice made soft.

'Now,' muttered Anna, 'How many fingers you got?'

I gaped at her. Anna stabbed me lovingly in the chest. 'Five – you great fool!'

'Five,' I whispered, 'five fingers I have.'

'One,' hissed Anna Friis, doubling one of my fingers back, 'and *four* make *five*.'

'Oh ja,' I said cheerfully.

'Count!' said Anna Friis, like the Goddess Freyja, getting terse with a tardy war maiden. I counted. 'Write!' commanded Anna. I shakily wrote. She counted my fingers – the magic ladder of figures on my paper grew. Then it was finished. I sat back, heavy with victory. '*I* go up – then you!' hissed Anna Friis. I watched her go up. She flipped back her lint-white plaits, and went, moving like a lynx, to join the serpent line. Her eyes narrowed. The line moved nervously forward. Several people smiled at her.

I raised my paper high in the air. I cried to Miss Gore in my true voice, cold as marsh-water, skidding through the glottal stops of the old language of Anna Friis and Astrid Westergaard. 'Look now at my country-man standing in your serpent line with her paper full of the right answers! Look now at your pupil Astrid Westergaard – writing out the true answers to the arithmetic of this school!'

There was dead silence. Anna Friis slowly drew one finger over her throat and jerked it at me. Eyes shining, neatly, swiftly as one of Freyja's war maidens moving on her cat's feet, I rose, slipped out, and joined the line, crashing into no more desks. The line moved nervously forward. Several people smiled at me.

The Looters

At night the looters came home, bearing their prizes, hungry for their dinners. And what were their prizes? The English language. They looted the English language and brought home their finds. Examples. Typical expressions. They showed off to each other. I sat at the table, beaming, all ready for my dinner and the talk. I could never keep up with the talk, but how I watched, how I listened! Astrid the spy, watching the other spies, much more skilful than me, for they not only watched and listened – they could read. They read everything they could lay their hands on. And I could not read. That was my shame, you know. I listened to the reading groups at school and I learned the words off by heart, for I too, was a looter. But when I looked at the words of my *Beacon Reader*, the words turned into thin black shapes, like Miss Gore. I gazed at them in despair. Nothing spoke to me from those words.

Tante Helga read novels and turned into the heroines. One day she was Anna Karenina, another day Madame Bovary. Always tragic and sighing. This, you understand, when she was not either the wild free Child of God, the Educator of the Nation, or a Vikingwife. She was very good at being a Vikingwife after reading too many of our Jutland ballads. She would gaze out of the kitchen windows at the Manawatu Plains, past the henyard, and make her eyes go stormy but resigned. Was she seeing the henyard and a portion of the Manawatu? Nej. She was back on the Jutland moors, gazing into Denmark's winter skies, longing for her sea-faring husband, who had failed to return in his long-ship.

The System

'Helga!' screeched my Bedstemoder, 'the food for the hens! Child – they starve!'

Outside the hens mourned in their yard, as hungry and resigned as Helga, the Vikingwife.

But this night, the night when my Reading Problem reached its crisis, into the room burst my Onkel Henning.

'Great Scott!' cried Onkel Henning. 'Dash my wig! By Jove! Food!' Then he paused. His military bearing lost its crispness. He did not know what to say next. Henning's favourite subject for looting expressions from was Major Gore, Miss Gore's broder. But Henning had not listened carefully enough to what Major Gore said in the privacy of his home when he clapped eyes on his dinner.

'Great Scott,' said Henning feebly. He gave up. He struck his hands together like a pistol shot. 'Now for our good dinner!' cried Onkel Henning in Danish.

My Fader's eyes sparkled. He bore down on the table. He stooped like a dwarf. He made his mouth as thin as a twist of string.

'We-ll, Sonny,' he drawled, 'yer goin' ter have yer tucker now, eh?'

He was Mr Lessington, the next door farmer again. Mr Lessington could not deal with Far's liveliness, so he called him Sonny, turning Fader into a milk-sop little Dunskie boy with blond curls. Every night Fader took his revenge and imitated him. 'Hope the tucker isn't crook tonight, boy!' he wailed. But Onkel Sven, the best spy, the most merciless imitator in the world, was not satisfied.

'Nej – nej!' he said impatiently. 'You got that a bit wrong there.'

He hunched up, he made his mouth as bitter as lemon peel, and he went one better. He shut one eye to give the impression of Mr Lessington's hat, of grey felt, drooping over one eye. 'We-ell, Sonny,' he drawled, 'yer goin' home to yer tucker now . . .'

My beam vanished, my mouth dropped open. For Sven, as usual, had gone too far. He had shut one eye, the one concealed by the invisible felt hat, but his one open eye glittered with ice that burned blue. Whose face looked at mine? Not Mr Lessington. Not Sven. It was the One-Eyed Traveller, the Beggar at the door, the Walker of the night. One-Eyed Odin was in our house.

Helga saved me.

The Bear from the North

'Don't be a silly muggins,' said Helga to Sven, copying the English slang. Then my Grandfather stood at the head of the table. He laughed. Then he sobered down. He raised a hand.

'Peace be in our house,' said my Bedstefader. And into the room came the two who never changed – my Bedstemoder, and my Moder. They set down the first of the food on the table. My Bedstefader raised his hands. 'Oh, God the Father . . .' he began. And Mr Lessington, Major Gore, flickered out like candle flames in the immense dark night stretching over the Manawatu Plains.

My Fader sat down by me while the others were washing up. He avoided the washing-up by reading me my night-time stories. He looted stories from the vast store of English literature and presented what he had found every night. Who was entertained the most? My Fader.

He hauled out *Tiger Tim's Annual*. Far loved Tiger Tim so much that I could not tell him the truth. I was afraid for Tiger Tim and his friends, the Elephant, the Giraffe, the Ostrich and the rest. For their Moder, Mrs Bruin, did not seem to have any furniture in her house, and she did not cook them good nourishing food. They spent their days wandering over the land, seeking food to steal. Bad food. Fruit cake, jam tarts and cream horns. Their teeth would fall out with no health-giving vegetables to eat.

Fader read the words in the balloons over the animals' heads in a rich, amused voice.

'Come on, boys,' he read, 'let us go and find Porky. Porky has gone into the woods with his hamper. Let us go and find him.'

There they were, at it again, war parties, seeking to steal more rich food. I glowered disapprovingly, but Fader read on, until the last picture was revealed. There were the animals, in a bunch, grinning. They had put Porky into a tree. They were looting his provisions. Tiger Tim and his friends each held a jam tart, eyes round as wolves. In each jam tart there was a large bite.

'Look at the bites – look at the bites!' said Far, as usual. 'They always have those jam tarts with bites in!' 'Then he rocked and chuckled while I gazed severely at him. 'Well,' he said, sobering down at my remote gaze, 'the *Girls' Annual*, and then bed.'

The Looters

I would cheer up at that announcement. For in the *Girls' Annual* there was a secure life.

' "The Fourth Form at Willendon",' announced Fader.

Ah. I gazed at the pictures all over again, of those glorious girls in their English school uniforms, ragging each other around the piano in the Common Room at Willendon College. If I could have been one of those girls, with glasses and buster-cut hair, rushing down corridors while bells rang, books dropped with a crash, whose friends were let down ivy-covered walls on ropes made of knotted sheets.

Fader read in a bored, remote voice –

'There was silence in the Junior Common Room at Willendon until suddenly Molly Lang looked up from her book and yawned. "To think we ought all to be out playing cricket!" she said. "Of all the boring summer terms." "Never mind!" laughed Enid Turner. She was sitting on the table trying rather unsuccessfully to put a passe-partout frame around a snapshot of a Sealyham puppy . . .'

I savoured those words in my mind like a secret drinker – 'sitting on the table' – what a jolly girl – 'Junior Common Room' – 'boring' . . . More useful words I could add to my store. I had not told anybody, but I was studying the English school girl. Out on the back lawn with my Sunday straw hat turned up at the back and down in the front and a ribbon tied around my lower skirt to turn it into a nineteen-thirties gym frock, I hobbled up and down with an old tennis racket, playing lacrosse with the Lower Fourth at Willendon.

'Jolly good,' I droned as I hobbled. 'Splendid shot! Oh, bad luck, Mavis!'

My Bedstemoder and Moder would admire me from the windows.

'Ah!' my Bedstemoder would cry, 'what movement – what a *dancer*! I could *eat* you!'

With ears flaming with embarrassment I averted my eyes from this unseemly un-English emotionalism.

'Jolly good,' I droned, hobbling doggedly on, 'play up, Mavis . . .'

'Now for your Reading!' said Far, ominously. We eyed each other. My gaze dropped first. I drew a deep, shaky breath.

'Fader,' I said, facing up to the music as I knew Mavis of

23

The Bear from the North

Willendon would do, 'I cannot read that *Beacon Reader*.'

'Come on – you're the cat whisker!' said Fader snappily, copying Miss Ogilvy, of the Fancy Goods Shop in the settlement. He sighed. He hauled out the grey book with the grey torch of learning on its cover. Far found the place and intoned like a prayer,

> 'c-an, p-an, m-an,
> h-op, g-ot, l-ot.'

He looked hard at me. 'Go on – go on,' he said, 'you read what you read me last night.'

I closed my eyes and huskily roared, 'Hop Pat. Hop Tom. Hop to the can, Pat. Hop to the can, Tom. Hop, hop, hop.'

I opened my eyes.

'You know it by heart. You've been listening to the other children,' said Fader. We gazed at each other, two looters of the English language.

'Kind God!' said my Fader in Danish. He looked glumly at the page. 'Who in his right mind would hop all day to that old can anyway?' he asked. He riffled over the pages, then stopped and read like lightning, his eye brightening. 'Now you listen, you listen!' he cried. He read in a full, triumphant voice, 'A big fat cook made a big fat pancake. Near the cook were seven hungry little boys. "We like big round pancakes, Mr Cook," said all the little boys. But the pancake in the pan said, 'I will not, not, not be eaten." '

Far turned to the end of the story and stabbed an ecstatic finger on some slanting words. 'See, see?' he shouted, 'Old Norse Folk Tale! Nor-sse!' he hissed in my ear.

'Norse?'

'Us,' said Fader simply.

He scrabbled around and found a pencil and paper. He drew a big circle on the paper. He gave it two eyes, a nose, a smiling mouth and two chins. He printed a word.

'Pan-cake,' he intoned.

'Pan-cake,' I whispered.

'Louder.' He pressed my fingers down under the word.

'Pancake!' I shouted.

Fader looked solemnly at me. Then he turned his face into a pancake. It grinned at me – it winked. That pancake would escape the fat cook, the seven hungry little boys and all the perils of the world, except at the very end. Then it would get too big for its boots. It would meet the fox, and snip, snap, the fox would eat it up. We laboured through the story and sure enough, at the end, we read,

'And snip! snap! he ate up the big round pancake. Yes, the pig ate up every bit!'

We peered suspiciously at that word 'pig'.

'Now that is wrong,' said Far. 'Now that pig should be a fox.'

The family gathered around. Voices were raised.

'Who prints that story?' cried my Bedstefader. 'This fine old Jutland story they have got it all wrong!'

I didn't care. I ran my finger over my picture of the pancake. I turned my face into a fat pancake.

'Pan-cake,' I said huskily, capturing each sound with a firm finger.

'Pan-cake! Pan-cake! Pan-cake!'

Arts and Crafts

There was always somebody doing something with thread in our house. Wool, linen-thread, gold and silver cord, cotton. Fingers flashed and stabbed at the knitting. Faces looked up at me and smiled while the fingers went on knitting.

'Kom, sit!' said my Moder, Tante Helga, Bedstemoder. I sat by them. 'Once a great King rode forth . . .' they started.

Why did the knitting and the stories commence together? From the weaving huts of Jutland. That was where the women went for the weaving, the spinning, the knitting. And while they did those things – the rhythm of their moving fingers made the old stories come. For hundreds of years they told the old stories of Denmark in the weaving huts. That is how I learned them. While I listened to the stories I watched the fingers. They knitted, they pulled threads out of linen for the drawn-thread designs, their needles flashed in and out of linen, embroidering field flowers, with their names beside them in single thread. Sometimes the flowers were Danish – but more and more, New Zealand flowers crept in. Wildflowers, flax and grass. I would go with them on the flower expeditions. 'Ah,' they would sigh, eyes intent, pulling here a shivery grass, there a spray of wild fuchsia. They would put their finds in a vase and watch them with narrowed eyes while they were baking, while they were drying dishes. '*Ah*,' they would say, eyes gleaming. Then they would sit down, and snip, snap, on the tablecloth, on the sampler, would come the same grass and flowers. Their embroideries changed. Nets of fine thread were woven to make a cobweb on the flowers and grass. Raindrops shone coldly in beads and sequins.

And my Bedstemoder made the river. Oh yes, she brought the river to life on fine linen. She made the raupo reeds, toi toi, waves, foam, long grass, and stones glittering on the banks. We found the stones, my Bedstemoder and I, with our kerchiefs tied over our heads, fluttering in the river wind under the great summer sun baking the Manawatu plains. We found little shells on the beach not far away, at Foxton. The long fingers of my Bedstemoder found them in the glittering sand and turned them over and over.

'The sea,' said my Bedstemoder. 'The sea!'

Her eyes turned a deeper blue as she looked at the long rollers streaming in. The family knew the ocean – they had come from it, they said. From Denmark. I looked for the hundredth time to see the fishtails on them of the Mer-Kings, the Sea-Folk. But that was when I was too young to know better. My Bedstemoder embroidered a ship on her river. She wove the rigging, spider-fingered. Shells winked in it.

'Look,' she said, 'the ship we came in. We danced and sang on that ship.'

I could see it all.

One day my Moder and my Bedstemoder gave me my first embroidery. A bunch of cherries on an apron for me. While I was making the cherries with needle and thread we had the winter floods. My Bedstemoder turned into a warrior queen when the floods came. She continually measured the rising water with her dressmaking ruler.

'Three feet!' she would shout, 'and still rising.'

The cherries came to life under my fingers on the day of the flood. I crouched over them in a patch of cold winter sunlight coming through a window. My needle flashed in the cold light as if it lived. It winked at me as it worked.

'You and I – and the cherries, eh?' it said.

I sewed the scarlet thread under and over to give an impression of plumpness. The cherries grew round and fat. I changed to green thread, and leaves and stalks grew like lightning. They shook in a spring wind.

The Bear from the North

At nightfall the flood water dropped.

'Two-feet-six!' cried my Bedstemoder. 'This house is saved!'

I cut the last thread and held up the apron. Living cherries grew on it. My Bedstemoder, restless with excitement, snatched up my work and held it to the light. Then she became very intent.

'Ha!' she said to my Moder. My Mor's cheeks flushed. She carried the cherry apron around with her.

'Look at my daughter's work!' she said to everybody – over and over again.

We draped it artistically over the sideboard while we ate our dinner and the flood water ran secretly away to the river where it truly belonged. We watched the apron as we ate. My cherries and leaves shook in spring winds.

At school I sat in my iron desk with a brand new pastel book open in front of me. Miss Gore held up a three-cornered stick, coloured brown.

'This is a pastel!' chanted Miss Gore.

'This is a pastel!' we chanted back.

Then we commenced the drawing. It was a castle. A difficult castle. You drew softly with the brown, the black, the white pastels. You worried it with grey pastel for the shadowing. Well, you want to know what my pastel castle looked like? A lump – flattened by siege – smashed by cannon fire. It was blackened with tears, it fell off the page. Miss Gore closed the tissue page over my pastel-coloured lump.

'No eye for drawing I can see,' she said.

'I can make cherries with the thread,' I said.

'No doubt,' said Miss Gore, and shut my book.

She gave us little sticks. They were the sticks the fierce visiting school doctor had poked down our throats. Spatula sticks.

'Now,' said Miss Gore, 'we are going to have a Parents' Day. We are going to make stick mats.' And she made one, in and out.

I struggled with my spatula mat. It fell to pieces. It was not thread – it was wood – too hard for the fingers to weave. In the end my mat was anchored with drawing pins.

My Moder came to the Parents' Day in her three-piece suit, the

Arts and Crafts

hat over one eye. She looked in silence at my spatula mat.

'Dearest God,' she said under her breath in Danish.

At home that night she gave me some crayons. Her cheeks shone pink with love and anxiety.

'We are going to draw an English garden for Miss Gore,' she said, 'to make up for that mat.'

We spent hours on that picture – copied from a lovely photograph in *The New Idea*. Larkspur, hollyhocks and crazy paving. A cottage garden.

'It will remind her of England,' said my Moder. 'It will remind her of her far-away homelands.'

The next morning I took the English-garden drawing, and the cherry apron, in a cardboard box to school. I laid the picture softly on the table where Miss Gore was sitting.

'An English garden for you,' I said.

Miss Gore looked affronted.

'An English *hus* from your lost homelands.' I said. Miss Gore picked up the picture between finger and thumb. Miss Gore was what we called an Ice-Maiden. No heart. She rejected her homelands.

'I think your Mother has drawn this for you, Astrid,' she said.

I shut her out of my life for ever. I left the cherry apron in its box.

Later that morning we were pushed into a line, with all our school books in our cases. We marched to another part of the school into an old, old classroom, that was built like a garden shed. That was the first classroom of all to be built, when children had not left the grass, the trees, the sky behind them. The windows rattled in the wind, but you could look out and see the world. In the room stood a young black-haired woman with an orange dress on. On the orange dress were printed pink tulips. I knew that orange dress, those pink tulips. It was my Russian doll, come to life. 'Children, this is your new teacher!' said Miss Gore in a voice as cold as Winter.

'My name is Miss Martin,' said the new teacher, my Russian doll come to life. 'Sit down – sit down!' We sat at wooden tables. No iron anywhere. Miss Gore marched back to fresh wars.

You know what happened in that room? Oh, kind God, it was a

new world You gave us that day. I showed Miss Martin my cherry apron, my English *hus*. Miss Martin held up the English-garden picture, the cherry apron, for all to see. For the first time, my people were honoured.

'Look at the stitches in those cherries!' said Miss Martin. 'The Danish are famous for their needlework. Astrid is learning all this!'

Oh, Miss Martin, Miss Martin, before somebody snatched you away in marriage, you made us see the world. Air, trees, flowers, grass rushed in upon our senses. We took deep breaths, we laughed, we talked. And the first Art and Craft we did for you was that model farm. Do you remember the model farmyard we made? Do you remember the sticky yellow raffia we cut into little lengths with our blunt scissors for the straw in the farmyard? And when I forgot myself, and called out 'Strå-strå!' you got everybody to listen and said for all to hear, 'Can you hear the English word 'straw' in that Danish word? The Danes came to England long ago. They gave us many words. You can still hear them if you listen carefully!'

How did she know that secret?

Oh – the Danes and the English were one people that day! One people!

Houses

There were two kinds of Manawatu Plains for me. The farmland, our Great Earth, that vast table-top stretching to the sky's rim. And the world of our settlement. On our farmland I wore my farmer's dress, brown shorts and shirt, sandals and a floppy straw hat. I sucked a grass stem in a seasoned sort of way between my teeth. My Fader made me a little wooden cart with thick wooden wheels. I sucked my grass and pulled my cart, looking the land and its weather in the eye. In that blinding light from the sky, skylarks screamed; I ran with my jolting cart and shouted back.

But in the settlement I crept in my patent-leather shoes past the dark houses with their green-stained paling fences cushioned by old yellowing carefully cut hedges. Cherry and I, our raffia purses in a ladylike dangle from our wrists, tried to peep into windows to see a fire in a grate, a rag mat, a kitchen cat. But under the white sky the settlement houses crouched, locked in darkness behind their bluebottle blinds, sending us back only our own reflections. Old fragile trees crouched close to the houses for company, the good farmland was cut up into squares and imprisoned there.

'No human being could breathe in those houses,' I said to Cherry.

'Wait till we get to my Granny's,' cried Cherry. '*Then* we'll be right.'

I could not tell her I was frightened of her Granny. It was the house. It crouched like a mouse behind its thick dusty macrocarpa hedges. In the gap along the bottom of the hedge, churchyard grass shook night and day in a bleak draught. The house hunched itself behind its hedges and peeped reluctantly into the fierce light through small, net-covered windows. I stood rooted by the gate.

'Just come *in*, come *in*, Astrid!' pleaded Cherry. The smell coming out of that house was of boiling meat. I could smell the poor slaughtered sheep. And the sound was the sound of a man's heavy boots coming down the passage, shaking the house.

A man's voice boomed, 'Which naughty girl needs a taste of my strap?'

That did it. I stood on the other side of the hedge, then I bolted home. I rushed inside and took great shivering breaths.

'Did you go to the house of Cherry's Bedstemoder?' asked my Moder.

'I have been to the house of the Trolde who boil the poor sheep,' I shouted.

'Nej, nej, nej,' said my Mor, angry with me. 'She is a very old woman. Her family were the first in this district. She knows this land, and she loves it here.'

But I didn't listen.

That year at school, we were all mad on the English thatched cottage. They were everywhere. We collected them with our eyes off calendars, off pictures hung over sideboards. In our heads we walked up crazy-paving paths littered with low-lying bushes of sweet-smelling English plants. By the cottage doors and windows those plants went wild. Roses climbed over thatch, delphiniums and hollyhocks grew as tall as church steeples. My Moder and the Tantes knitted their brows over the satin-stitch required to get the exact feel of the hollyhock. French knots were required to suggest the topmost buds of the delphinium.

And one day Miss Martin announced the Competition. We were to make a miniature garden. A cottage garden! In a box, or in a dish. My skin shivered. I rushed home.

'Wait, wait,' urged my Moder. She got out the *Stitchcraft* and slowly and reverently turned to a fancy-work picture, to be worked by ladies; for about a year of afternoons, we thought. Everything was there – the low-lying bushes, the roof-climbing roses, the dizzy spires of the delphinium, the hollyhock. And, in addition, there was a sort of garden below the level of the surrounding paved paths, with formal flower-beds, and a garden seat, and a sundial!

'Sonken garden,' said my Mor in a low respectful voice. The picture was dotted at the edges by garden soil – Far's exasperated thumb-prints.

He was striving to create a sunken garden for my Moder out of the rich Manawatu soil. She would not allow the *Stitchcraft* to be taken outside and left to flutter in the wind while Fader strove to dig out the good soil for a sufficient hole in which to insert the paving stones through which the low-lying plants were to artistically grow. In pauses in the digging, Fader could be heard tiptoeing into the house with his boots off, swearing softly, to check on the sunken-garden basic plan from the *Stitchcraft*. But the hole had slowly filled with water, and one day there were two ducks . . .

'You make a sonken-garden miniature box?' wheedled my Moder. My eyes shone. All through dinner I planned the measurements of sunken gardens until poor Far put his head into his spade-blistered hands and groaned. We would send straight away to Messrs Cadbury and Sons in England, I announced, and request them to send post-haste that book of push-out cottages and barns that you won when you had collected fifty of their lead farmyard creatures, concealed in every tin of Cadbury's Cocoa. I was sure, I added, that I had sifted through fifty cocoa tins with my fingernails . . .

In school next day I made my simple request to have a team of Mud Manufacturers for my Plan.

'Who is going to make mud with Astrid?' asked Miss Martin. At that word 'mud' two hands waved timidly in the air. Chrissy Hamilton and Mickey Woodley. They had no head for figures – or anything, come to that – but they always sought out strong leaders to give them orders. Me!

I led them grandly to the fountain. It was going now – or dribbling – but you can't have the world. I had to wait while the Mud-Manufacturing Team gravely stood in a line and had a drink. We weren't supposed to take cooling swigs from the fountain, but when we managed to snatch one we called it fountain nectar.

The Bear from the North

When my Mud Team was slaked, I organised them into the Mud Assembly Line. My idea was that each child should produce a simple block at fast speed, four walls and a paved floor, which would dry to rock-hardness. We could then plant the low-lying, sweet-smelling plants. Chrissy Hamilton and Mickey Woodley, smiling humbly, set to work with a will rolling out little balls.

'Slabs,' I said in a strong voice, drawing slab outlines in the air. They went on briskly rolling out balls.

'Cannon-balls,' said Mickey proudly. Then a voice cut through our dream.

'Westigid,' shouted the Headmaster. 'Leave that fountain *alone*. Replace that dirt immediately.'

With hearts leaping like salmon we shovelled back the dirt.

'Where we goin' to make more marbles for you, Astrid?' asked Chrissy in her hoarse voice. Mickey suddenly grinned at me and flung out his hand like a ferret from a bush. In it lay a host of cannon-balls. He whisked them under his shirt again. Miss Martin poked her head outside our classroom door and delicately blew her whistle at us.

'Drop them, drop them,' I gabbled, plans crashing into ruin. Chrissy and Mickey scuttled back to the classroom, doubled over the mud-hoard clutched to their bosoms.

After school I walked into our sitting-room like a great, enraged, defeated general.

'All they want to do is to make mud marbles. Cannon-balls!' I roared. 'They will not make slabs.'

My Mor took me on to her lap and rocked me back and forth.

'Tss,' she said through her teeth, 'tss, little Astrid.'

'Peter the Great,' said a General's voice in the corner, 'made thousands of men build his great city of St Petersburg from the marshes of Novgorod.' My Bedstemoder regarded me with a mad emperor's cold eye. 'Dig! he said to those men – *and they dug*!'

'Well,' said my Moder in the gasping voice she had when something was unexpectedly amusing, 'you will have to order your men to dig that mud and no more fooling with cannon-balls.' Then she shook and shook.

'Dig!' I said in Peter the Great's cold mad voice to my Mud Team.

Houses

'Dig slabs, not cannon-balls.'

'We'll dig the mud for you, Astrid,' said Chrissy, smiling and smiling, 'oh, *yes!*'

Between them Chrissy and Mickey made a gigantic heap of fresh cannon-balls.

'You should see my miniature garden, Astrid,' said Cherry in her soft little voice. 'My Mum made me a real little path from stones and a real little pond from her handbag mirror. You scatter dirt around to give it the natural look. I am making ducks and bullrushes out of glitter-wax.' I ground my teeth with wicked envy. Cherry edged closer.

'My Granny,' murmured Cherry, 'knows how to make miniature gardens. She has *things* for them. *Old* things.'

My mind filled up with poor slaughtered sheep boiling in pots and voices roaring. Which naughty girl needs a taste of my strap?

'Oh yes,' I murmured in a traitor's voice.

'All you need,' said my Fader for the hundredth time that Saturday, 'is a little more command over your men.' He gazed hopelessly at me. Then he leaned his head ingratiatingly to one side. 'Chrissy! Mickey!' he piped, 'slabs – squares – not cannon-balls. Alley-oop, men!' Then he lit his pipe and leaned back. 'Alley-oop, men!' he said, and gave the sudden helpless snort that always came before his hoots of laughter.

'Astrid,' said my Moder sternly, 'put on that blue dress and the patent-leather shoes. We are to go on a visit.'

My heart jerked. I was not so good with the ladies at the tea-parties. The formality of the cake-stands and the little embroidered napkins sliding off the knee made me sweat so much that my Moder had to let me go outside. I usually ran around the ladies' lawns a lot and took in great gulps of cooling air.

Far proudly let us out of the car in the main street of the settlement.

'Which ladies are the Cats' Whisker?' he asked. We walked gravely past the Regal Picture Theatre and the paddock next door with its poor dying town-grass and past the evil billiard parlour and past the War Memorial, and before you could say snip-snap straight up that side-street to Cherry's Granny's house.

'*Now* Astrid,' said my Moder and hauled me up to the front door. Feet rumbled through the house, its walls shook and my heart died. The door opened. There stood Cherry's Granny in a good black dress. She was about the size of a walnut.

'Karen West-er-gaard!' said Cherry's Granny. Her voice was exactly the sound of mouse's feet whispering over walnut shells. 'Ast-rid West-er-gaard!' said the mouse voice.

How did she know our names?

'Goddag,' I boomed, sweating like a horse. My Moder led me in.

'Say hullo to Dad,' sang Mrs Taylor. A little black bent man stood by a draped curtain doorway.

'Hullo, Miss Astrid,' he said.

'Goddag,' I whispered, waiting for the strap.

'Karen,' said Mrs Taylor, 'you are more like your mother every day.'

How did she know my Bedstemoder?

Mr Taylor wrung our hands.

'Sit down, sit down,' he said.

We sat in dolls' chairs. I peeped at the room. It was crammed with furniture and ornaments. And in the fireplace there were old filmy ferns. Mrs Taylor followed my eyes.

'My Mother grew those,' she said. 'She always got ferns from the bush and grew them inside.' She looked at Mor. 'Your mother and my mother,' she said, 'always could grow the ferns from the bush.'

'What bush?' I asked, too surprised to be polite.

'The bush all over here,' said Mrs Taylor. 'They cleared it.'

She pointed up at the wall. There were old coloured photographs of green and lemon-coloured people. Very worn-out people.

'They were pioneers,' said my Moder. 'They were strong people. They were here long before we came from Jutland.' Her voice shook, and then steadied.

'Shall I get it?' said Mr Taylor impatiently.

'Our tea,' said Mrs Taylor, placidly folding her hands in her lap. 'That is a nice idea, Dad.'

Mr Taylor tiptoed across the room and all the ornaments tinkled in chorus from the shelves. I looked at the china cabinet. It was crammed with treasure; mother-of-pearl, cut glass, silver glinted at me. He opened it and slowly, carefully lifted something out. He set it gingerly on a little table by my chair.

'We thought,' said Mrs Taylor, 'for Cherry's little friend.'

On the table lay a meat-tin. And in it was a garden made for mice. A little path made of shells ran straight up to a pond; a handbag-mirror pond, with earth scattered around it to give it the natural look. Two china ducks floated over their reflections. Behind it was a trellis with white wax bridal-flowers on it. And at the back was a little china teapot, shaped like a thatched cottage.

'See that *house*,' cried Mr Taylor. 'That comes from a teaset. Very good china, that was.'

'Oh, Astrid,' said my Moder, and her voice shook, 'no more cannon-balls.'

I dragged my eyes away from my cottage garden and looked up at those green and lemon-coloured people in the photographs. I gazed in deep content at the pioneers of our Manawatu.

Guy Fox

That November, when I was not quite seven, the teacher at school told us of somebody named Guy Fox. He had lived long ago and had sought to destroy the king with fire. We had a night in his memory, she said. November the fifth, when we lit fires to honour him. Why would we do that? I asked her. To remember traitors, she said.

I trailed home, turning over her words in my mind.

'On November the fifth,' I announced at dinner, 'we make fire for a fox called Guy.'

My Fader hooted. He put his face down to mine and enunciated carefully, 'Guy *Fawkes*, Guy *Fawkes*! He nearly blew up London.'

'How do we light his fires?' I asked.

My Fader's face worked as it did when I grew older and joined in festivals, the memories of our Danish history – celebrated with fire. At the tomb of the Valiant Soldier, for example, when the cannons held red and white carnations in their mouths and the soldiers marched holding torches that flared in the night. The fires on the shores when the sun danced at midsummer. Iron baskets of fire in the snow to light the traveller to the houses of his friends.

But there were no festivals in New Zealand when the sacred flames held back the dark.

'I will give you a shilling,' said my Far, 'to take to the store to buy the fire-crackers. And we will take our crackers to the farm for the night of November the fifth.'

The farm was the oldest Westergaard farm, on the road outside

Palmerston North. The farmhouse was so old that all the door latches were made from wood. Everything in it had come from Jutland; black wooden furniture and so on. When I was very little and sleeping in that house, voices in the downstairs passage had woken me in the middle of the night. My oldest Grandonkel, Flemming, was talking in Danish.

'Prepare the food,' he was saying, 'for old Ole Hansen. He has come to this house, cold and hungry. Rise, rise and give food to our guest.'

Outside my door suddenly appeared a tall woman, holding in one hand a branched candlestick. Three candles burned in it, casting shadows over the walls. The woman, my Grandtante Ingeborg, stood and fastened the collar of her long black dress, with her eyes fixed on the kitchen door. Then she turned her head.

'Kom,' she said abruptly, like a dronning, a queen, and moved up the passage. And after her hurried her daughters, Ingrid and Mette, heads bowed, swiftly twisting up their hair, ready to greet the guest in the night. The candle-light flared, and fell away into darkness, into sleep.

In the morning, an old tramp raised his red eyes to mine from the breakfast table.

'Godmorgen, Astrid Westergaard,' said the tramp, looking at me to see how much Westergaard I showed in my face. My Grandtante Ingeborg pushed me sharply in the back.

'Godmorgen, Ole Hansen,' she prompted me.

'Godmorgen, Ole Hansen,' I murmured, eyeing him.

For he was not Ole Hansen. He was One-Eyed Odin in disguise, the Visitor from the Night, greeted with food and fire in silver branches, to warm his winter bones.

When we got to the farmhouse, it was nearly dark. In the orchard, a bonfire flared. Around it darted figures. Faces shone in the flames. They were my cousins. They were suddenly in front of us, and stood to attention.

'Godaften, Onkel, Tante, Astrid,' said Finn, the oldest. The other cousins smiled.

'Godaften, godaften, godaften!' shouted my Fader. 'Where's old Flemming now?' People surrounded us. There were our families, dressed in their coats, laughing and pushing the children forward.

We were late. Hands grasped mine, lips brushed my cheek. Where was my Moder? Into the house with the Tantes she went, carrying our baskets of cakes for the feast. Whose feast?

'Guy the Fox!' said a voice over my head. 'Fires for the Fox!'

I looked up. Standing black against the last of the sunset was my Grandtante Ingeborg. She clasped my hands in hers. They were restless with excitement.

'In Denmark we see the fox,' she said. 'Over the snow he goes. The fox . . . and the wolf. Kom, kom,' she said. 'Up on the veranda while they get ready.'

She stood me on a stool by the veranda rail. She pressed me against her side. She had a story in her ready to be spoken; I could feel it racing through her blood.

'In the winter in Denmark,' she said, 'we light fires in iron cressets in the snow, to welcome travellers home.' Her r's rippled in those words.

'This is a true story,' she said, as she always said. 'Once long ago in Denmark a man set out to visit his friends. That *cold* winter in Denmark. Frost was on the ground; frost was in the sky. His feet rang on the hard road. He was afraid. No man did he see; no living thing was there. He look forward to see his friends, all that laughing, all that talk, all that food! But he could not see the light from their window saying, here we are – come in, come in. By and by he was afraid. He prayed to God that he was not lost. But he was. He stopped. And then he see something move. A *shape*. You know what he see?'

'Nej,' I whispered.

'A dog. A great grey dog. And – oh – it was so sad! That big dog was lost too and so glad to have a good friend at last. It pressed close. Ah, says the young man, my friends have sent you to guide me to their home. The dog whimpers, and that man he puts out his hand to pat it and its coat is the coldest thing in all the world. But it keeps close to him and leads him on, and by and by they come to a little bridge that the man knows well. The dog looks up and its eyes are of fire. It keeps with him to the end of the bridge. Then there is the friends' house. This good Christian man looks down – and there is no dog there . . . And you know what his friends say when he gets to their warm house at last? That was no dog, they say. That was a *ghost*. A ghost of a wolf. The last wolf killed in Denmark – one hundred years before!'

We gazed, satisfied, at each other. She let my hand drop. 'Now!' she said, deep in her throat. And into the air soared fire, white stars fell back on the summer-leafed trees and bathed them in ice-crystals.

'Ah . . .' sang the grown-ups, heads back, drinking it in. Somebody pulled at my hands.

'Astrid! Astrid!' said the voice of my cousin Finn. In his hand he held a stick that spat stars. Over it his eyes looked at me, gleaming like the Fox, gleaming like the Wolf. 'Ild!' he shouted. 'Fire!'

I took the stick of stars and held it up. I shouted 'Ild!' and brought my festival fire to the Manawatu. And in its fox-fire I saw the last wolf of Denmark, racing over the paddocks to far lands. Racing into the darkness, on over the snow falling on Jutland.

On, on to the North.

Gods and Heroes

You never knew who you were going to meet on our farm when you went for walks with Mor and Bedstemoder. But I could handle those people they told me about, for they met them rather casually, and they were quiet people. Longlegs the cat came with us on our walks. He bored through the tinker-tailor grass like a submarine on the floor of the ocean. When he lost sight and sound of our walking feet he leapt high in the air, sighted us, and dropped back on course again over his sea-floor.

'Where's Longlegs?' I kept calling. 'Longlegs, Longlegs.'

'He has a friend,' said my Bedstemoder. 'That other cat. Together they draw Freyja's chariot through the air as she rides over the world and looks after the green things of the earth.' I spun around and looked at Longlegs. He looked blandly back. In one eye-blink, he was Freyja's cat. In the next, Longlegs purring over his good breakfast after his long night's journeying. But I could handle that change. I liked quiet, quick changes.

Like the flicker-flame. My Moder told me about a hero called Skirnir who had gone to see his girl in her farmhouse up north somewhere. Round that girl's cow paddock had danced the flicker-flame. But Skirnir was up to dealing with things like that. 'Jump, my horse,' said Skirnir, and, one-two, clean over the flicker-flame jumped his horse. Then they both looked back – and the flicker-flame was gone! A farmer was there instead, sitting on a mound, looking at them from under his broad-brimmed hat. Who was that farmer? Golden Thor, the protector of farmers. I was used to him.

But Tante Helga plunged out to meet gods and heroes head-on,

Gods and Heroes

dragging me with her. And I hung back. I dug my toes in. She was worried because I wasn't keen on the sea.

It was simply that I disapproved of the loose life that went on in the sea houses, the beaches. After the floor was swept in the morning, the dusting done, the fire built up in its hearth and the dishes put away, the house should have been able to build up its own life, its own gleaming silence, surrounding all its people and giving them rest and new life. Well – the sand just drifted in and lay where it wanted. You trod on it, you ate it, it dulled the windows and the dishes. The house became restless. Instead of the deep stillness of the land in the long afternoons, the sea never stopped moving and talking to itself.

I stood in it up to my waist and watched it sternly.

'Splash!' cried Tante Helga in her blue swimming-suit with the straps coming down. She giggled and hurled a fistful of water at me. It hit me like a blow. I stayed hunched like a bad-tempered seagull, my mouth and eyes screwed up as if I was eating lemons.

'Splish-splash!' cried Tante Helga, hurling more water. Then she gave me up. She put on a solemn face, put both hands together in an attitude of prayer, and started her swim. She was like a paddle boat churning along. Then she jumped up, closed her eyes, and reverently splashed sea-water all over herself.

'The sea heals all wounds!' called Tante Helga. 'The salt cleanses our skin!' Several other swimmers stood up and watched her. She let loose several more handfuls of magic sea-water over her head. Then she noticed the swimmers silently watching, and changed into a gay flapper.

'Jolly good swimming!' she cried. Nobody answered.

But the most shameful thing was yet to come. Tante Helga also believed in the sun's mighty healing rays. While I stood on angry guard, searching the distance for signs of approaching beach-walkers, Tante Helga enthusiastically stripped off the blue swimming-togs and lay down, sopping wet and naked as a fish, on the sand behind a small fringe of marram grass.

'Lie down, lie down, lille Astrid,' she urged, foolishly snug behind her thin grass screen. 'Let the sun *get* at you.'

'I don't want it to!' I wailed. 'Tante Helga – there's a dog coming up the beach, and a man close behind. Tante *Helga*!'

'He will soon pass by,' came soothingly from behind the marram grass.

'Tante Helga, Tante Helga – there's a whole *family* coming up the beach – with a dear little old woman. Their grandmother! Tante – get dressed quickly.'

'They will soon pass by,' came a drowsy murmur from the marram grass. I stood guard and glared at all beach walkers. Then, at last, Tante Helga dressed in a flash, did some deep breathing, and opened up our healthy lunch. I was as limp as an old handkerchief with relief, and Helga knew it.

'Do you know about the goddess Gefiunn?' asked Tante in her deep, special story-telling voice. I stiffened. I did not want to *know* about the goddess Gefiunn.

'She made the first land,' said Helga casually, 'from the sea.' Silence. 'She was a great singer and harpist. And she had four strong sons. She wanted them to have land for their farms, so she asked the king if he would let her have as much land as her bulls could plough in one day.'

'What was she doing ploughing with *bulls*?' I asked loudly. 'Everybody knows you can't plough with bulls.'

Helga changed into Madame Montessori, very low and peaceful.

' "Ah, well," said the king to Gefiunn, "that won't be much! You go right ahead." And Gefiunn turned her four sons into four strong bulls and ploughed the sea.'

'You can't plough the sea,' I said, and looked at it as it heaved itself about on Foxton Beach.

'And they dragged a piece of the land away, and anchored it to the sea floor,' said Tante Helga.

'Well?'

'Don't you want to know *which* piece of land?'

'No.'

'Zealand in Denmark,' said Helga triumphantly.

'We're in New Zealand now,' I said.

'I think the same thing happened with New Zealand,' said Tante Helga. 'A hero called Maui dragged it up from the sea. On his fishing-line.'

I stood up.

'His line would have broken,' I said severely. I did not help Tante

Helga with the packing-up of our healthy lunch.

We tramped glumly down the Foxton Beach to where the beach houses began on the sand-hills. We were going to see a Danish family. The mother was Tante Helga's friend. She was such an upright woman, Tante Helga kept saying, so strong and laughing.

We went to a sea house that was on top of the tallest sand-hill. It was terribly dark inside. There was sand everywhere. And standing in a room, with her head nearly touching the ceiling, was a woman with a big voice.

'Goddag, Helga Westergaard,' shouted the woman. 'Whom have you brought to see me?'

'Astrid,' said Helga proudly. She pushed me in front of her. 'Say thy name.'

But I was dumb. That woman was so tall!

'See,' said the woman. 'I have made thee a jelly.' She held out a tin bowl to me. I could see clear through the red jelly to a dark-red flower painted on the bottom.

'Eat thy jelly,' wheedled the woman, 'and the flower is yours.'

I was so foolish. I did not honour the food she was offering her guest.

'I only have jelly for my pudding,' I said darkly, 'at my dinner-time.'

There was dead silence. Helga and the woman looked at me.

'You will eat the jelly for dinner,' warned Tante Helga.

The jelly lay in its lair and watched me. I will not eat thee, I said in my head. We will see, said that jelly, and was silent.

Then the room filled with people. The woman's name was Mrs Hagen and she had very tall sons and one silent datter. And in one minute, snip-snap, the table was covered with food; cakes and smørrebrød and coffee.

'Eat, eat,' urged the woman. And we all sat down. The sons grinned at their Moder, said not a word and fell on the food. But I would not eat a morsel. That woman put things in her food, I knew it. I would be changed for ever if I ate a crumb.

Helga and Mrs Hagen began the gossip, like knitting-needles flying back and forth, each voice doing a row.

'How is thy kindergarten faring?' asked Mrs Hagen.

'Good, good!' answered Tante Helga, seizing a cake. I primly watched her. The sea had changed her. She ate like a giantess.

'Do you beat the naughty children?' called Mrs Hagen, and laughed, showing her big teeth and some cake crumbs on her tongue. 'I beat my sons, oh yes, when they were little. Wicked little sons I had!' shouted Mrs Hagen and clapped the tallest one on the back. He choked. All the sons laughed.

'Else they should beat *me*!' hissed Mrs Hagen, thrusting her face into mine. I drew back in alarm. All the sons laughed again. They must be those wild Norwegians, I thought, pelting each other with pine-cones and going to sleep on the table with their feet among the supper bowls.

'Well, tell us, how is the kindergarten now?' prompted Mrs Hagen, leaning keenly forward.

'Working in happiness,' said Tante Helga in a rich waterfall of descending notes.

'That is so good,' breathed Mrs Hagen's daughter, clearing up some empty plates. She is the only true Christian soul who sits at this table, said the voice in my head. A good Danish girl, not given to shouting.

'Hah!' said Mrs Hagen, 'I would whip them. I would drive them to their work!' Her sons laughed. I glanced sharply at her. Mrs Hagen glanced back briefly, then rose. 'Walk – walk now,' she said. 'I will get the dinner. And lille Astrid will help me.'

The others moved slowly to the door. 'Go and smell that sea-salt!' she called, and they went. With sinking heart I watched them go. Tante Helga left me to my fate.

Mrs Hagen suddenly whipped the tin bowl on to the table in front of me.

'You eat my jelly?' she asked.

I looked up, at bay. Mrs Hagen looked at me.

'You do not like the sea,' she said. 'You do not like the sea, lille countrywoman. You do not like its violent motion and its noises. But in Denmark, and here, we are close to the sea. It is all around us.'

I looked severely out of the window – and then I saw the sunset. It covered the whole sky. Great red seas washed the world. Mrs Hagen leaned over and held out a piece of smørrebrød. 'Eat my food of the sea,' she said, and her eyes burned, washed me in love. I took one reluctant bite, and my mouth was flooded with such salty bliss that my skin shivered. 'Fish,' said Mrs Hagen. 'Fish in its sea-salt.'

The red light flooded the room. Mrs Hagen stood and faced the sea and laughed. Her body stretched and grew until she towered over the red sky and the glittering sea. And I saw – I *saw* great bulls shouldering the waves and a red-gold woman striding into sea-spray, raising one arm, calling to me – her child – to spring into life from the ocean floor, into the first seas of the world. The roar of the Baltic, the roar of the Tasman filled my head. A long, sighing, whispering roar.

The Mound

Well now, what was the playground of that school like, eh? At first look, it was all concrete. Concrete steps rose up to concrete tennis courts. More concrete steps rose up to a ghost of a fountain – a fountain that was dead. One day I would make it go. I would turn on its tap that I would find deep under the ground. Up would go its feathers of water. The birds would fly singing through the spray. Huzzah! the children would shout. We would throw away our books and melt into sun-spray.

It was forbidden to walk on the lawns. It was forbidden to climb the trees. But the sad dark green New Zealand bushes had little hollows in the middle. When you had friends you sat in the hollows and told each other life's secrets. I had my friend – Anna Friis.

'Kom!' said Anna Friis impatiently. 'I will show you everything there is to see.'

So we went into the school hall, where the dead were.

It was a sad Valhalla. From outside came the distant sounds of the living warriors, testing each other in their war games. Inside were the signs of the valour of their fathers, the Warriors of England and New Zealand.

A flag hung from the roof, its ends nibbled by mice.

'Cannon fire,' murmured Anna's voice, cold in my ear. I backed away from that battle banner. She took my hand. 'See the deaths of the English,' said Anna Friis.

We went along a row of pictures. General Woolf died on a rocky plain. Lord Nelson lay elegantly dying under beautiful ship's sails and the sad eyes of his comrades. Captain Cook walked sternly through prancing black men. One had an axe raised in the air. Captain Cook's reproving eye was on a warrior prancing higher than the rest. Control yourself, said Captain Cook's reproving eye. He did not look behind to see that axe. A modern field marshal looked at us from behind his moustaches. He was asking us to join the next war.

But Anna was leading me to the greatest picture of all. I stood stock still in front of it. There they were, the Maori people, falling on to the shores of New Zealand, ribs showing, eyes staring, mouths open. A little sail on their canoe was in tatters. Some of them were already on the beach, heads down, digging for pipis, and no wonder. They must have paddled all the way.

'This is a most wonderful land for dying,' I told Anna Friis mournfully.

'Ah,' said Anna Friis. She stood on one leg. We looked at the Maoris landing on New Zealand's bleak shores. I pulled her sleeve. Excitement made my voice hoarser than usual.

'Did we come here, to die early?' I asked.

Anna looked thoughtfully at me.

'You mean to see something secret?' she asked.

'Ja!'

'Kom!' she said. She grabbed my hand. We darted out on to the concrete. Rushing towards us was the usual battle charge of boys. Their big boots crashed, their eyes stared at nothing, their mouths gaped. Every play break they started The Run. They just ran on the concrete, round and round the brick school. If you got in the way of The Run, you died. I clutched Anna's hand and pulled back.

'The Runners!' I shouted. 'The Runners!'

Anna held my arm, she stepped out in the middle of the running boys. I shut my eyes. Then I opened them. The boots were faltering, skidding, coming to a stop. In the middle of the runners stood Anna, as tall, as cold as Hel, Queen of Death. Facing her stood a tall boy with Anna's eyes. He had come from nowhere, his face was still, watching. His mouth curled in its smile.

'Kjeld.' said Anna. 'Goddag.'

'Goddag,' said Kjeld Friis. His slanting blue eyes took me in, and went to sleep again. 'Goddag, Astrid Westergaard,' he said in his dream.

'Goddag, Kjeld,' I whispered. I looked at his dark blond hair and his golden skin. Anna jerked my arm. Kjeld led the way. We walked through the boys like two dronninger. Then I lost my tallness, my soft Jutland stride. I stumbled along.

'Anna,' I said, 'you stopped those boys' boots running. Now how did you do that, Anna? Anna? How did you do that?'

Anna glanced briefly at me. I slowed down. I walked with the slow swing of my Bedstemoder, of my Moder.

We went through the trees and over the fence into the pony paddock. I stopped, entranced. The grass of the Plains was here again, running in the wind, freed from bells, whistles, raps with rulers and hands on heads.

'Mmm,' I said, plunging my face into tinker-tailor grass, washed with milky peace.

'Up!' commanded Anna. She pulled me up like a sack of potatoes. She set off sternly through the grass, ignoring the fortunes that could be told on the tinker-tailor grasses blowing around her. I stumbled after her, snatching at good fat grasses that could be chanted up later in the warm privacy behind the shelter shed.

'Observe!' said Anna Friis, pointing. Clutching my grasses, I steadied on my feet, dizzy in that rippling sea. Far off over the paddocks a great mound of earth rose up. The grass ran up over it and down the other side. I blinked and sharpened my gaze. Did the grass on that mound run more secretly, more swiftly? I waited. I will tell you something. Now and again, if I stilled all my senses, slowed my breathing, there would come a message from that land to me. As if a voice spoke one word. When I was grown, I thought, I would understand its language. Now I could only gape, my mouth open, clutching my tinker-tailor grass bundle.

The wind swooped down on us. The paddock boiled, but the grass on top of that mound ran evenly, steadily, from end to end.

Anna moved towards it. I followed, dropping my tinker-tailor grass. We stood together in the wind. I looked up at Anna Friis' face. She was watching that mound, eyes intent, listening.

'Long ago,' she said, 'sea wanderers came here. In the long-ships.' The grass hissed.

'In our dragon-ships?' I asked. She slowly turned and looked at me. And in her eyes I slowly recognised the rapt blind gaze of the sea travellers, the Viking men. Our Danish people had those eyes when they remembered – other days.

I looked over the mound, over the paddocks to my house. There it was, the Jutland barn, built by our families, faithfully down to the last nail blow, to the design of our great red barns in Jutland. Its end rose up in the air. Its end was a prow, the dragon-head of a great ship, its eyes empty now, but one day, one day, ready to fill up again with fire, with blood, at the sight of new lands. I looked at Anna Friis.

'Anna,' I said, *'what is in that mound?'*

'Kings,' said Anna. 'The silver Kings who came from Denmark. And their long-ships, their silver hoards and their swords and axes of Thor. All are in there.'

The grass thrashed, the wind roared, and the Jutland barn raised up its dragon-head on the waves of air, scenting the new land.

'Anna . . .' I said.

Then I looked back at the school fence we had come through. And there, standing motionless, steadily watching us, stood Rangi Katene, the tall silent Maori girl from Standard Six. Her hair whipped about in the wind.

I looked at Rangi, then up at Anna. They both ignored me. They had eyes only for that mound.

I turned and looked at the school. It seemed smaller. By its back door a cluster of little girls crouched in a circle. One of them was holding up a doll. What were they chanting in their game?

> Rock-a-bye-baby,
> On the tree-top,
> When the wind blows,
> The cradle will rock . . .

The wind bellowed from the sky and blotted out their voices. I turned my back on them and watched the mound. And I was as tall and watchful as the other two. There we stood, the people who had ridden the endless seas in ships with prows like dragons. Rangi Katene, Anna Friis – and Astrid Westergaard.

My Bedstemoder

My Bedstemoder is uneasy, and so am I. We are visiting a new sea, a harbour. The Wellington Harbour. We are both having a little holiday, with our older second cousins. That family which has left the Manawatu Scandinavian settlement and settled in Eastbourne.

We are used to a different kind of land, strong flat earth under our feet, the broad river, and *our* sea, that is an ocean, on the west coast of the Manawatu. We know that ocean's moods. We know its morning calm when we boil the billy and the sun burns the tender leaves of the lupins. We know its afternoons, when the wind gets up and hissing sand stings our ankles. We know its long mournful echoing roar. Distant figures, onkels and tantes, sit solitary on sand dunes, gazing as if they can never have enough of it.

But I am slowly being seduced by this sea's mermaid's beads, its sea-lettuce, its pauas gleaming under the coins of light that glide over the surface of rockpools.

We look suspiciously at the house's bush garden. The bush is full of tiny shivering ferns, elf-haunts. The grass is not good for feed. It is fragile; bits of shells gleam in it here and there. As if the sea stealthily covers the lawn each night when we are all asleep. I drink the water from the taps with lips barely open. That water comes from a creek in the bush. You could swallow an elf, a lille spilopmager, if you did not take care. At home I gulp the artesian water with wide-open mouth. It tastes of grass and dry earth and sun. All things I know well.

At eleven each morning the cousins take us down to the beach.

My Bedstemoder

They carry long brilliant beach towels and Japanese sunshades. Old ladies walk down with beach wraps over their swim-suits. Their blue-veined legs end in thin rubber beach shoes. Not my Bedstemoder. She wears her long black dress, the pointed shoes with the buttoned straps, and a large black hat. She walks like Fate down the hill to the beach. She sits uneasily on a small sand dune, her hands darting and stabbing ceaselessly at her knitting, while she watches the athletic young men carrying gay, screaming girls – the flappers – into that gentle water. I push a beach ball through the water and busily swim, one foot carefully planted on the sea floor. The smell of that sea-wet rubber ball is paradise. But my Bedstemoder would like to wear her furs and her black toque and tap her silver-topped cane along an esplanade, gently promenading, as they do at the Foxton River, on the hard river sand, where our beach houses were.

Back in the steep, toppling house, in the afternoon, regularity, ceremony asserts itself. There sweet peas sweetly branch in fluted vases, the black marble clock with the golden dolphins at each end ticks time away. Bedstemoder pours English tea from a silver teapot, settling the room, and us. She speaks Danish, listening to the cousins' conversation with steely attentiveness. She wishes to be reassured that no carelessness has crept into their speech. This elf-bush, this gentle sea has not blurred them into soft ways.

But she need not worry. The same food seethes on the stove, settles in the stone cold larder into its true flavour.

So, this morning, we are washing up, my Bedstemoder and I. She is looming over the sink like a great sailing ship, absently washing – absently lifting our sud-covered cups and dishes and almost letting them slide off the bench on to the floor. All day she has drifted rather than walked about the house, looking fixedly out of the windows, staring at Wellington Harbour, but seeing – other things. My Bedstemoder is seeing other faces, other shadows today. And so am I. She is remembering; I am discovering. Outside, the sun blazes on the bush in the garden, the blue hydrangeas have a look of marble, of old, water-cooled stone. We are both not here, and the cousins part as we drift by, and join together again, a murmuring, shining sea.

This morning has been the same as usual. The same dark, cool

The Bear from the North

kitchen, the same fruit and cream in a blue lustre bowl. The bowl is the sea, the cream is a sea-king's marble palace far under the ocean. Something peppery is cooking on the stove, someone's bitter coffee cools by my place at the table.

The night before, an old cousin has told me the story of the Little Mermaid. She tells stories as if she has just heard them; as if, in a second, golden people, firebirds clashing burning wings, will come into the narrow room, the walls will melt, we will see the great world. They all *begin* matter-of-factly.

'On the shores of the cold North Sea lived a foolish fisherman and his wife . . .'

And how do they end?

Never trust ambition. Count your cheeses before you go to market.

This morning, I have gone with my Cousin Sven down to the Eastbourne Beach, where the Italian fishermen are pulling the long net. How can the net be so long, the harbour so vast? My cousin grips my arm, one of the fishmen is singing with long sweeps of his voice that fly straight to the sun.

'Listen!' he says fiercely. 'He sings with his whole self.'

The fisherman falls silent. They let me help pull the rope of the great net; dripping sea-lettuce from the Little Mermaid's ocean garden strains through my fingers, ice cold. We go to Mrs Stimson's dairy, brown bread in a bag and one of Mrs Stimson's iceblocks, white, green and brown to lick, stinging, in one's mouth as we trail home. I look again at the Little Mermaid's pictures, in the book; drapery flowing from her dancing body, over marble pavements into the cool sea that longed to comfort her burning feet. What was the lesson? In my cousin's bedroom a photograph of the Little Mermaid's statue shows me her lost brooding face gazing at the sea behind her.

And now my Bedstemoder and I are washing up, slowly, slowly after lunch.

'Tell me,' I ask, drugged with the sun on the sea from the kitchen window, 'when you were a little girl.'

My Bedstemoder darts two gleaming eyes at the summer

My Bedstemoder

harbour, as if it is her enemy. She rests her hands, always splayed delicately sideways when she rests them on the sink. She has been remembering many things today. They come in a rush. They have been in her for all her time in New Zealand and now they have stirred into flame again.

'The ship,' she says, '*our* ship . . .'

She looks the sleeping harbour fiercely in the eye, daring it to forget its past.

'That beautiful ship we come in,' she says. 'My brothers, my sisters, my Moder, my Fader. We all grown up. We have Danes and Norwegians and Germans and Poles in that ship. They make a choir. Such strong beautiful voices. They sang when the storms came – to give us *heart*!' (Only she says it not like those bare words. Her voice is like sea water, up and down and quickly slurring.) 'There is a figurehead on that ship. A girl with a fish-tail. Her face is like mine, I think. She seems to laugh when the great green waves hit her. So I laugh too. For was I not child of the north, a sea-child?'

She dramatically turns and faces me.

'Ja,' I answer, 'I can see you doing that.'

'Good!' she says briskly. 'We have fever, and we cure it. We have a ship's hos-pi-tal and a good doctor.'

The soap bubbles are drying on her hands, but she ignores them.

'We *arrive*!' she says. 'With all our banners flying their dragon's-breath, and our Dannebrog flying too. The sails thunder in the wind, we dressed in our best. And everyone has a streamer to wave to the New Zealanders when they wel-come us. Over there!'

She points to the distant Heads. Innocent waves gently cream the rocks. But I see the ship. I *see* that ship.

'Did you sing?' I ask.

'We *sang*!' she declares, slapping down a hand on the damp bench. 'But they wouldn't let us land,' whispers my Bedstemoder, gripping my shoulder, eyes dark as winter seas. 'They say – "You go to that island" – a little man in a boat with a speaking-trumpet. They hear us speak. They say we are Russian. They never hear our Danish language before. You know *that*?'

Arms flung out, there stands the Norne, the teller of her people's fate.

'An island?' I ask.

The Bear from the North

'That!' she cries, pointing at Somes Island. It sleeps on.

'In boats?' I ask, stupidly.

'What else?' she demands. 'A storm blew up. We had to carry the people who have been sick. So weak. Through the waves. And sheds to live in. With no glass in the windows. And then, above these houses here –' she waves at the neighbours' houses – 'just trees. Forest. And it burned that night. Howling winds and howling flames. The end of the *world*!'

I look horrified at the harbour. It winks languorously back. But I see that ship from the north, from the far ice lands, the Dannebrog cracking its white and scarlet, sails streaming in the roaring wind, and my Bedstemoder, the girl coming out of the sea, with the Little Mermaid's cold Nordic sea-eyes, clambering up slippery rocks.

'Three weeks,' she says, 'we stay. We have school, and church. We have four Danish pastors and a good teacher. And our choir. And in the end we *land*. At the wharf. All of us, and our pastors, dressed so fine. Our pastors blessed the city from the ship's deck. So they see us at last, the people from the north, still so brave.'

We are both still, side by side, staring at the sun on Wellington Harbour.

'Quarantine,' I say.

'*What* you say?' she demands.

'Quarantine. To get rid of the germs.'

'We have the finest ship's hos-pi-tal . . .'

'The last of the germs,' I state doggedly, 'had to die.'

'Ah?' she says. '*So*.' And lapses into the summer silence in the kitchen.

'What was it called?' I ask, in our dream.

She says a long word in Danish.

'Tell me,' I repeat. Does she say, '*The North Star*'? Or do I dream it? I lay my head on her shoulder. She brushes my hair back with a soapy hand.

'It was so cold that winter,' she murmurs. 'The ice –'

I see the secret Northern lands locked in the whisper of winter ice, swans' wings creak overhead and are gone. I see the black rigging of the ship, brittle with frost. I see my Bedstemoder's face, as tender, as wistful, as the Little Mermaid's looking back to the land she has lost.

But there are feet running up the back steps. She suddenly moves.

'Not *North Star*!' she cries. '*Lille* one – *Terpsichore* – the dance! Ha?'

She dances backward to the pounding on the back door, swinging her skirts at me and laughing. She flings open the door to angel faces, the Italian children, offering us open suitcases gleaming with fresh fish, marbled, sparkling with seawater from the beautiful Wellington Harbour.

'Anna!' she calls. 'These *naughty* ones have brought us the lovely fish again – in suitcases. Whatever *next*!'

Arbor Day

My Onkel Henning believed he was a tree. Oh, ja. He was a part of Nature, he said. When everybody else came home to dinner with the gossip, Henning's gossip was of grass, the bush, and Nature.

'Ah!' he would cry as he unfolded his dinner napkin. 'Today walking along the road I saw this grass that I well remember in Denmark. It is like a cloud in which the body can sink down and rest. I just saw a lille patch of it, you know, locked behind the fence, and before I could stop myself, snip-snap, I was over that fence and into it. I lay back and it soothed the whole system.'

'Ah . . .' would breathe Tante Helga, that other child of Nature, 'was it that grass called Mist Grass, Henning?'

'Fog Grass,' my Bedstemoder would say briefly. 'Yorkshire Fog' – rolling the r's.

'Ah?' Henning would ask, his eyes turning that milky blue they turned when confronted by the more brutal realities of cow farming. 'I call it Cloud Grass.'

'*Cloud* Grass,' Tante Helga would echo. And she and Henning would drop away into a trance and let their dinner grow cold.

Onkel Henning took me for little expeditions into the bush. While I fought the undergrowth, Henning strode along looking up at the trees.

'Totara,' he would intone, 'rimu, kahikatea. In Denmark,' he would say, 'the beech trees stand by the shores. They cast their long yellow leaves on to the ground when autumn comes, turning the sands into gold.'

Arbor Day

'*Gold*, Henning?' I would cry, struggling through thickets of supplejack and bush lawyer. 'Real *gold*?'

'Listen to the trees,' Henning would say, stopping dead in his tracks.

We would gaze at distant treetops, high above our heads. They would be golden in the sun, housing birds and so on.

'What do they say, what do they say, Henning?' I would nag.

'Do not break God's silence in the forest!' Henning would command, one finger uplifted. I listened and listened, but the trees' words were only for Henning's ears.

That was until I discovered the oak. The oak tree stood in the garden of Cherry Taylor. We lived in it for a whole summer. It was a very clean tree, no bush lawyer catching in the hair, no vines to strangle the climber. We sat in its branches and ate its young leaves. Cherry's outraged Moder handed up our lunch to us one day. It was a pie filled with golden syrup, but I closed my eyes as I ate, and pretended it was cherry pie. Cherries as red as Cherry's cheeks. She looked like a cherry. I could have eaten her. But that was an old wicked Viking thought, so I did not tell her, in case she was startled.

We picked up hundreds of acorns and took them to school in little cardboard boxes. Miss Martin snatched them up as if they were Henning's golden beech leaves, and waved them at us all.

'Nature's bounty!' cried Miss Martin.

She learned words like that from *Arthur Mee's Guide to Nature's Wonderland*. Miss Martin read us bits of Arthur Mee and we took fire from his enthusiastic commands. We were to go for Nature Walks at the weekends, and write all our observations down. We were to sharpen our eyes and seek out the spindle-berry, the horse-chestnut, and the magic wings of the sycamore. We ranged the paddocks, burdened with notebooks, tobacco tins and pencils. We found none of those chestnuts, sycamores, and so on. Once I found a kind of nut in a thistle-head which was most delicious food. So all I could write in my notebook was –

'1 Thistle-Nut. Useful Food. Eaten.'

And in the spring I wrote–

'Saw 5 lambs and 1 daffodil.'

But while we were searching, Cherry and I would look up at the dark patch of bush by the creek. It stood without moving and looked silently at us.

Arthur Mee never told us what to look for in there.

The oak tree smelt of fresh washing drying on the line. It rocked in the gales and we rocked with it, perched in its branches like two birds.

At school, one day in June, Miss Martin faced us with the news.

'Arbor Day is coming!' she cried. 'We are to plant trees! Groves of trees!'

Cherry raised her hand. I knew what she was going to ask.

'Are we to plant oak trees, Miss Martin?'

Miss Martin's cheeks turned a deeper pink. She clasped her hands. 'The oak,' she called, 'the ash and the bonny green bay!'

Ah! We gazed at her, wondering where you got the seeds of the bonny green bay. We knew why rapture was within her. She was going out at the weekends with a young man with a beard who was going to be a dentist. They scandalised the district by tramping over the cow paddocks, dressed in great boots and shorts and shirts and jumpers, bowed down by bundles tied on their poor backs.

'Rucksacks,' said Onkel Henning knowledgeably, 'for when they camp out in the wilds.'

Henning was taking my little boy cousins out for real camps in the bush. They told me that they slept in one tent, and Henning snored all night. And in the morning they cooked scones and pancakes on an iron plate over a fire. Henning wore a long white apron and turned the scones over and over and told them the stories of the Maori, who had lived in the bush in the olden days and cooked their breakfasts in deep pits lined with fire, but did not make the scones or the pancakes for their breakfast. The little cousins' eyes gleamed when they told me all this.

But at school Arbor Day rushed upon us. We talked of nothing but trees. We made trees out of paper, cardboard, twigs and plasticine. We learned the habits of the oak, the ash, the elm and the yew. Cherry and I kept our oak tree in our hearts. We shook in the gales, we grew acorns and leaves in our hair.

The trees were to be planted in the Recreation Ground. The whole school was to have Arbor Day to plant them. The whole day

Arbor Day

making trees! On Arbor Day, the Headmaster came into his own. We were to march to the Recreation Ground carrying the tree saplings. That Standard Six drummer boy had been practising all week. He stood to attention by the school gate. He sounded the death-rattle on his drum, and the seniors lined up. And down the path Miss Martin's class marched to join them. Prepared. Miss Martin's fervour had ignited us. There she was, marching at the head of our line, dressed in her boots, jumper, bush jacket and shorts, rucksack bulging with lunch, Arthur Mee and the First Aid Box. Her legs were coloured red and blue with the cold. And we marched in our Arbor Day outfits, best dresses, hats, and in some cases, patent-leather shoes.

The Headmaster surveyed us. He was dressed as usual, in his grey.

'Well, Miss Martin,' he said, in his grey voice, 'ready with your camp-followers I see?'

Miss Martin gave her jolly laugh, taking it on the chin as usual. We laughed too. But soon sobered down.

'All over this Dominion,' shouted the Headmaster, the fervour of the British Empire in his eye, 'school children are marching with trees to plant for our Nation! And on every tree that grows will be mounted a metal plaque; with the name of the boy – *or* girl – who has planted it.' Cherry Taylor and I looked at each other. Our eyes filled up with groves of oak trees, belonging to us for ever more.

Then we marched, school bags bumping our legs, down the endless gravelled road and down, down, into that Pit of Hell, the Tainui Recreation Ground.

For it was bottomless, edged with terrible old black macrocarpa trees that endlessly hissed stories of the Maori Wars in the wind that never stopped sighing down there. High above our heads rose the cliffs that belonged to the river, when it had run there, thousands of years before. And in the macrocarpa trees stood the Maori Meeting House, so old that its timbers were crumbling into the ground. Children whispered that framed pictures of dead Maori warriors hung in there and that they were *in* there even now; they hadn't died at all. Miss Martin's class, patent-leather shoes pinching, sidled past. On the gable top of the Meeting House a wooden warrior stood brandishing a spear. His dead eyes gleamed their paua shell gleam at us. They watched us all the way.

The Headmaster braced himself behind a long row of sad little trees lying on the ground. The oak, the ash, and the jolly green bay.

'By the right,' he roared, 'ad-vance!'

We stumbled forward. Into our hands were pushed two trees, roots dropping mud. The Headmaster raised his whistle.

'On the whistle-blast,' he intoned, 'you will follow your teachers to the line of planting!'

There they were, at their war games again. We stumbled over the rough ground, clutching our trees, to where big boys waited, resting on their spades that had dug the graves for our trees. With two strokes of those spades our trees met their deaths.

We advanced with more trees and snip-snap, they were buried again.

At last the Headmaster blew his whistle. We came to attention.

'Lunch will now be eaten!' he commanded. But there was Miss Martin, smiling and beckoning us.

'Follow me, dears!' she called. We trailed after her, through a rusty iron gate, and into an old, cracked tennis court with a little pavilion leaning to one side.

'Here we will have our picnic!' cried Miss Martin. We laid down our coats and sat on them, fussy as old women, and opened our lunches. But Miss Martin had a paper bag in her hand. She held it out to Cherry and Cherry slowly, reverently drew out a chocolate fish.

'For our Arbor Day,' said Miss Martin. We slowly nibbled our fish, making them last. Then we looked up.

At the foot of the cliffs, by the Meeting House, an old Maori woman stood, dressed in black, watching us. Behind, the bush stood, black against the cliff. Under us its roots silently pushed up the tennis court into bumps, into cracks. The pavilion leaned to one side, its foundations undermined. And the wooden warrior on the Meeting House roof raised his spear, his paua shell eyes, guarding the holes, the caves deep in the cliff, where they had buried their dead in the old days, the warriors of the Maori Nations of old New Zealand. Their unsleeping eyes watched Miss Martin's class eating the chocolate fish.

The Garden Party

When I was nine I fell in love with the land. I tried to know all its secrets in one breath. I found out that you have to learn its secrets, an inch at a time. And just when you think you know one of its seasons off by heart, it changes. It becomes a different person. I remember the moment when I began to learn the land's secret off by heart. I was lying face down on our back lawn with my eyes closed. It was spring, but we had had enough wind to dry the ground. By an enormous effort, I managed to remember the smell it had when summer baked it. A smell of wind and jointed grass, of water and stone and bread and butter and cheese.

'Mmm,' I murmured, and rolled over on my back and opened my eyes. Black against the spinning sun stood my Bedstemoder, holding an oven cloth, looking at me. I squinted up at her.

'Did you see the sun dance?' asked my Bedstemoder. 'Lunch!' said my Bedstemoder.

That night before I went to sleep she told me another story of old Denmark. That night she told me of the Norner, the Fate-Tellers. They were tall women, she said, who walked with no sound. You could tell who they were by their eyes. They wore long, finely woven white veils hanging from head-circlets of silver. They went into the Danish camps on the eve of battles. They read magic signs in the land, in the air and in fire. And they told the King what his battle-fate was to be. He had to bear that prophecy alone, being the King.

'Were they sisters?' I asked.

'Ja,' said my Bedstemoder, 'they each knew what the other was thinking.'

'What else did they know?' I asked.

'How the harvest would turn out,' said my Bedstemoder practically. 'They were at the Spring Ceremonies in Jutland. They knew all the dances and songs.'

The next day I tiptoed into my Bedstemoder's room to have a good look at a picture that was on the wall in there. No people in it. Just a boat – a black boat with a faint suggestion of a dragon-prow, floating on silver water by black river reeds. The reeds were in flower. The boat was untied, floating with oars ready. On the other side of the wide silver water lay another country. The boat lay silently waiting for its passenger.

Who was that passenger?

At school that week, Miss Martin told us the news.

'Soon it will be summer,' she said, 'and this year, we are to have a garden party.' There was dead silence. Miss Martin cried, 'They are all the rage, quite the mode in the Old Country!' She waved a picture. Grey and black ladies and gentlemen looked gravely at us from under felt hats shaped like drooping snowdrops. A little girl with a dress straight as a pencil with frills hobbling her knees had one eye closed, squinting savagely at us. A tent drooped in a garden that needed weeding.

'Their tent's falling down!' called out Georgie Thompson. 'They need to tighten the guy ropes!'

'It is a special tent,' said Miss Martin, 'a tent in which ladies sell things which one can make.'

She opened our map to Correct Living, *The Teachers' Monthly Guide*. ' "Dainty favours for the bazaar can be fashioned from quite humble materials",' she read. 'We will make them out of scraps and ribbons begged from our Mothers!' cried Miss Martin, warming up, 'and you will be dancing on the lawn, in crepe-paper costumes!'

We gaped, thunder-struck, at her. To walk on the lawn meant instant death from that grey Headmaster. He locked lawn-wanderers in his office and they were changed for ever. They smiled like fools and spent the rest of their lives banging out the

The Garden Party

blackboard dusters on the concrete and weeding the tennis court.

'We are to practise,' cried Miss Martin on a rising trumpet-note, ' "Gathering Peascods and Strip the Willow". And now we will get to work on the details of your costumes!'

I sped home, chanting to the rhythm of my marching feet, 'Gathering Peascods – Strip the Willow!'

I burst through the back door, and there, turning around with the same movement from the bench, were two strange tall women with the same eyes. 'Ah!' cried my Bedstemoder in her high singing voice that she had when visitors came. 'Look who has come to be with us. My sister Bodil!'

Tante Bodil wiped her hands on her long apron and leaned down and kissed me on both cheeks – the left side – the right side.

'Goddag, lille Astrid!' she cried in my Bedstemoder's voice. 'Hvordan har du det?'

'Godt, tak,' I mumbled, and did my bob.

'Crepe paper!' cried my Moder. We were waiting for our dinner. Out of the corner of my eye I watched the two sisters out in the kitchen, stirring the sauces, stooping to peer in the oven. They worked as one woman, each one knowing what the other was going to do next, with no speech. Their hands flew like birds, chopping, stirring; then resting, sleeping birds, on the other's waist, or shoulder.

'You dance, in crepe paper?' insisted my poor Mor.

I wrenched my eyes away from the kitchen. 'We dance the Gathering Peascods,' I chanted, drawn again into that dream of dancing on the lawn.

'Peascods – peascods – peascods!' muttered Far. He went irritably over to the shelf for the dictionary. 'Peascods!' He snapped his fingers as he whipped over the pages. 'Ah! Aertebaelg . . .' a comfortable sound like water rippling over stones. And then the English word. Fader pushed out his lips in a popping shape. His eyebrows rose, his nose pinched with the effort. 'Pea-pod,' he said in a mincing, tiny voice. 'You gather the pea-pod in this dance,' he said, 'but we don't grow peas here.'

'They did so in England,' I said, 'long ago.'

'Dancing in paper?' said my Moder.

'It is the mode,' I said in Miss Martin's voice, 'quite the thing in the Old Country.'

'*Their* Old Country,' said a voice in the doorway. My Bedstemoder bore in the soup. Tante Bodil bore in the hot bread.

'Ribbons,' she said, 'garlands, you should wear. The dresses with the fullness.'

They set down the food. They faced each other, one hand lifting a skirt, one hand making a still shape in the air.

'So!' they said together. First to the right, then to the left, their bodies moved. Tall, their feet making no sound.

I watched the Norner dance.

'Ribbons and spangles, scraps and sequins!' sang Miss Martin. She peered at the heap of our Mothers' sombre scraps. 'Now – we begin!'

Oh – we began. Do you know what we made?

Pompoms. Round and round a cardboard circle with a hole in it went the wool. The scissors sliced a circle, we pulled tight, and there, dangling, was a magic pompom.

Raffia, damp and dead, a thick smell, but growing nowhere, I think, in the Manawatu. Round and round, another cardboard circle, our fingers straining to keep it flat.

'So that the teapot may not tip to one side!' called Miss Martin. My teapot-stand was purple, to give a little fire to the tea table.

Last, last, came the kewpies. They smiled and smiled at us without blinking, while we made their evening dresses. Skirts for them, rolled with pencils along the edges, glued on to the fat stomachs of the kewpies, bound around with silver ribbon. On their shoulders we sprinkled silver glitter. Then we leaned back and gazed at them, and sighed at their beauty.

We practised the dancing in the school hall.

'One and two and one and turn!' roared Miss Gore. She marched up and down the scene of battle, twirling a long ruler, nostrils flaring, a terrible field marshal. We fell about. The boys would not touch the girls' hands. The enormous, thick black record spun round and round on the gramophone, and ran down, groaning. 'Halt!' Miss Gore dared us with fierce eyes to break ranks for more bread rations, while the Headmaster, who had appointed himself Gramophone-Winder, quelled the big boys against mutiny, and bent down for more winding. Up came the music again, a tiny orchestra with no breath left after its long journey to us from England.

At home I walked through the movements in front of my puzzled family.

'One and two and one and turn!' I roared in Miss Gore's voice.

'Ha!' cried my Fader. 'This is the way you pick those pea-pods!' And leaping to his feet, he whirled my Moder round and round. She danced with no hard breathing. Chairs scraped, and before my eyes my whole family turned into different people. Aunts and uncles galloped up the room and down again, with no hard breathing. With laughter and joy.

On the garden-party day I wore the brown crepe-paper dress. Already the sweat under my arms was making it melt. But I wandered, crackling, all over the lawns, and looked inside the tents. Strange ladies of the district were at work, arranging our dolls, our teapot stands, our pompoms to look their best. The silver kewpies stretched out their arms to the world and smiled and smiled. I remembered the dance on the lawn and swallowed a bolt of excitement.

In our circles on the lawn, we stood and waited. The new green leaves on the trees by the gate hung, limp, in the still air. But through the fences, stretching away to the horizon, stood the grass of the Plains, heavy with seed, waiting with us. The Headmaster, a surprising pink rose in his button hole, wound up the gramophone.

We started. And then I looked up. Walking through the tents on feet that made no sound came the tall women – Tante Bodil, my Bedstemoder and my Moder. They stood, the three Norner, and looked at me. Something came into me. I let go Georgie Thompson's hand and danced. Oh, they were the steps of the Peascods dance that I followed, but some other dance came over those movements. I raised both hands and I danced for the land, standing, waiting to be honoured, through the wire fence. When the other children turned once, I turned three times. I avoided Miss Gore's outraged glare and danced, looking at the land. And the land spoke to me. It went through me like a lick of flame, and my body became someone else's body. And in that moment I was the land. My hair was the grass, my skin held its smoothness, its shine. When the music stopped, I curtsied, not to Georgie Thompson, but to the land. And the grass moved once, and was still again.

I looked up. My Bedstemoder, my Tante Bodil, and my Moder were looking at me. Their eyes flared with welcome. But not to me. They welcomed somebody else they had thought they would never see again.

The people clapped. Under that vast sky it sounded like birds' beaks striking together.

Birds. Ravens. Odin's Ravens.

The Followers

When my eyes were sharp enough to watch the world, I started to look at the ground my feet walked on. I found that my body, then my head, were at ease when my feet found earth that they liked to feel. Dry ground and tree roots, for example. I made a house on the edge of our pine trees. On one side of my door was a pocket of earth held firm by a lacing of pine roots. In that hollow I laid twigs and cones for my house-fire. I sat cross-legged in front of its imagined flames, transparent in the quivering afternoon air. I looked out at the summer land and felt its dry rich earth in my bones.

'Hjem,' I said. 'Home.'

But it lacked stretches of water for the swans to fly home to.

'Ah...' said my Bedstemoder, and sank down on the starved grass at the edge of our river. Children screamed and sent flurries of sand flying down the distant sand-hills. Jaws clamped shut to keep the water out, eyes starting from my head, I slowly and grimly dog-paddled past her.

'Wonderful, Astrid,' she said absently, using her r's and v's. But her eyes looked always beyond the sand-hills and the sliding children to where a giant breathed over the sky. 'Listen...' she said, and half closed her eyes. 'The ocean...' Her voice darkened and lingered over that 'o' in ocean. She had often told me that our families had come from Denmark in a ship with sails like swans' wings; that they had come from the ocean. I often pictured them clambering on to the rocks of New Zealand, combing their wet hair and shaking the salt water out of their ears. For even after long years of living on land, their eyes showed from where they had come: ocean-blue and cold, reflecting great depths and distances.

'Nevertheless,' said my Bedstemoder, 'I miss our *lakes*.'

I stood up, a shivering river-maiden, and cast a look at the ground where she sat. Black sand flashed its mica through the innocent grass. Its salt would scorch the grass roots and dry them into straw. Grass needed fresh water to grow into good feed for animals.

My Bedstemoder waved a sad undulating hand. 'The reeds, the fresh-water lakes, the swans, and so on . . .' she said, remembering that land left far behind.

Danmark. Hjem.

So I watched Danmark, for signs of my true hjem.

'Ha!' cried Onkel Henning, handing round the Kodak snaps at the Sunday afternoon family gathering. He had just come back from Denmark and wore a new Danish suit to prove it; a cycling costume in tweed. He had a new modern hair-style to match – combed straight back from his brow, to facilitate speed.

'I cycled all over Jutland!' said Onkel Henning proudly. 'And where does my good old bike lead me one morning? Straight as an arrow to Ansker's farm.'

'Straight to Ansker's farm,' chorused all the cousins, and pursed their lips and nodded at the photograph, each in their turn.

'And what do I find?' demanded Onkel Henning, opening his arms wide. 'That very same milk-can that Ansker left by the gate – twenty year ago!'

'The *same* milk-can, Ansker!' chorused the cousins, beaming at Ansker.

Ansker beamed back, and looked long and hard at the snap; then he secretly wiped his eyes with his fingers – one-two – and handed it to me.

'Ja,' said Ansker, and looked at his feet.

I looked at Ansker's farm to draw it into my bones. I saw a farmyard with thatched white buildings on one side. I saw a tall windmill as white as milk. I saw a flock of geese as white as the windmill racing towards a boy wearing a linen cap, a blouse, long pants and clogs. And under his clogs was Jutland earth. As black, as sticky as dark chocolate.

'Too much *water*,' I said.

'Ja,' said Ansker, and secretly wiped his eyes again.

At that time I was deep into jigsaws. So Onkel Henning brought me back a Danish jigsaw. It was a very hard one; a thick wooden puzzle with a picture of strong grass and water. There were large birds flying over a wind-bent tree. Swans. The water was a little lake, with reeds. As I slowly pushed the wooden shapes into place, I sank down in peace in that jigsaw land. I breathed slowly and deeply. I heard those swans scream in the Jutland wind.

My Fader leaned over me and pushed a piece of the strong grass into place.

'Lyng,' he said. 'Moorland heather. It is red and springing. One may lie upon it as a person lies upon a fine mattress and hear the birds call one to the other.'

'I am going to find my own land *here*,' I said. 'My land is going to have this kind of water for the swans, but with good grass for feed for my animals. Not too wet and not too dry. I am going to live there when I am an old woman,' I told him. 'I am going to sit at the door of my house all day and watch my grass and my water and my birds.'

'Ja,' said my Far. Very nice and peaceful I am sure.' And he went out to dig in his vegetable garden.

When he came in again he washed his hands and sat down to help with the jigsaw puzzle. He told me that he had come to the conclusion, out among the vegetables, that I was going to be an arch-conservative – either peasant or aristocrat. It didn't matter, he said, as they were both the same, clinging to all the old ways.

As we pushed jigsaw pieces about I tried to decide. I liked the idea of an elegant shabby house with large rooms to think in. But then there was the neatness, the divine simplicity of the peasant's cottage; the sweeping of its two small rooms with a twig broom, the frugal portion of soup simmering over my peat fire. But all I really wanted was a place to live in so that I could sit at the door and see that sky, that grass, that water and those birds. My swans. They would tell me all they knew and I would write everything down in

The Bear from the North

a special notebook. Then I would know all the secrets of the world.

But Tante Helga introduced us to the Holy Grail, and Anna Friis took over the Boy Scout Troop.

Tante Helga became concerned about our lack of knowledge of British culture, and one day she descended upon us, waving a small red book. It was called *King Arthur and His Knights*.

Oh, those knights were so delicate! They had long, bony faces; too fragile, it seemed, to hold up their great iron helmets. And they lived in another kind of land; a very damp, tangled land, full of thickets and woods and over-grown streams. They spent their lives drifting about haunted glades, and never seemed to eat good nourishing dinners. They spent a great many sleepless nights on their knees in woodland chapels woven out of sticks. Sometimes, if they struck it lucky, there was a small bonfire on the altar. *That*, said Tante Helga, was the Holy Grail. They tried to find it all their lives, and worshipped it.

Anna's eyes shone. I tried to get back to the jigsaw puzzles, but she discovered the Boy Scouts. It was the Scout Church Parade that did it.

Anna and I had gone to the settlement to see if there was another wedding at the Anglican church. We had once seen a bride arrive in the back of a Ford, with her father proudly driving. When she climbed out she was as pale and solemn as her white veil under its band of violets.

'Violets, eh?' murmured Anna into my ear. 'She couldn't afford wax orange-blossom.' But the violets went with that church in its dark trees, and the moss-cushions bordering the brick path. And the houses in the settlement matched the church, dark and closed-up in their silent trees, with sometimes of an evening a rich, secret smell of stew hanging in the air.

We hung uneasily around the church gate. Anna thought she heard the organ playing. Then, far down the road, we heard a bugle! And there, bobbing unevenly over the gravel in the road, came a host with a banner held high. Resolutely, four by four, marched the Scout Troop. Their poor legs looked so tender in those great shoes and socks, but it was their hats that enraptured Anna, and their banner. White-faced, bleak-eyed, they halted to a high-

The Followers

pitched wail from their leader. Then they removed their hats and held them under one arm, *just as Arthur's knights did*, before they entered their woven-twig chapels. They went inside, banner in a sort of trail, the organ pealed, the door closed, and the organ died away to an interesting mutter. Anna, moving with no sound, scrambled up the church steps and into the vestibule. After a bit, she darted back again.

'They've got the Holy Grail in there,' she said, eyes flashing. 'It's burning away like hang on the altar.' She leaned towards me. 'They're doing their vigil,' hissed Anna. 'They'll be kneeling there *all night*.'

My heart ached. Poor things – their knees would get so sore on that Anglican straw matting.

The next Saturday, Anna suddenly appeared at our door, Cherry Taylor in tow. Anna seemed very excited.

'Come for a ramble,' she cried.

A ramble! Cherry said nothing at all, but steadfastly hung on to her Nature Notebook, pencil, and Nature Collection Tobacco Tin.

We went over the paddocks towards the reclaimed sand-hills. When we got beyond the cow paddocks the grass was dry and thin, with warm hard earth underneath. My senses sharpened. I was always looking for that lost jigsaw-puzzle land. Cherry mooned along, looking for white butterflies, but Anna marched forward, impatiently scanning the horizon.

Then we saw them – a long line of Boy Scouts unrhythmically marching towards the first hill, ignoring grass, clouds and white butterflies.

'Come on,' called Anna. 'Let's catch them up!'

Cherry and I stood stock still. But Anna went loping off. We had to follow. She had the lunch; we had only the lemon juice.

We caught them up just when they were vanishing over the hill. The Scout Leader looked at us in horror. It was Cyril Pennyfeather.

'Girls!' yelled Cyril in his cracking voice. 'Speed it up, chaps!'

The Scout Troop moved into a brisk shamble. Anna ran like a deer, and attached herself proudly to the end of the Troop. Cherry hung back.

'Astrid,' said Cherry in a low, urgent voice, 'I can't go on.' I stared at her. 'I've got a hole in my pants!' she wailed. 'They'll see it, Astrid. All those boys will tell everyone Cherry Taylor has holes in her pants. I cannot march with them.'

'How big is it?' I asked practically.

Cherry abruptly whipped up her skirt and bent over. By squinting fiercely I could just make out a hole the size of a pin in her neat fawn pants.

'It's only the size of a pin,' I said. 'We'll have to follow Anna. She's got the lunch.'

Cherry trailed far behind. When I looked back she was attempting to trot with her skirt wrapped firmly around her knees. I caught up with Anna.

'March . . .' she said dreamily. 'Keep up!' She had the look of Tante Helga rapt in one of her visions.

'What are they doing?' I gasped, trying to keep up.

'Carrying on a Quest,' said Anna in a low voice. I glanced back. Cherry had now hitched her skirt between her knees and was attempting to run. I hoisted up the lemon juice and waited for her.

The Scout Troop moved even faster, and broke into a raucous song. We didn't know the words. They, and Anna, vanished over another low hill.

When we reached the Troop they were encamped, if you can call it that. They had spread all their eatables out on the grass, and were chasing each other through some patches of gorse. Sometimes one of them trod on a pat of butter they had opened and abandoned on the grass. Anna was sitting on the edge of the clearing, watching with shining eyes.

'They are exercising,' she murmured, 'just as the knights of old exercised before battle.'

You could have, I thought sourly, as I opened our squashed lunch, a little too much of Arthur and his knights for the healthy growth of the mind. Before she fell to eating her lunch, Cherry fussily tied her skirt into a granny knot in front.

'I'm going to tell my Mum on you, Anna Friis,' said Cherry. 'She doesn't like little girls who chase after Boy Scouts.'

'Huh!' said Anna, bolting her food with one eye fixed on Cyril

Pennyfeather. He was aware of that eye.

'Tracking, chaps!' he called. The Troop formed into a jostling bunch. 'Hares off!' he shouted. 'Me and Russell!' Russell was so exhilarated at this enigmatic command that he cast his cavernous scout hat on to the ground. It fell over the roast of beef he had brought – cooked by his loving Moder. Surely he should have cooked it himself, on a stick over an open fire?

'You can be hounds,' said Cyril carelessly in our direction.

Anna sprang to her feet. But she was too late. The whole Troop, idiotically baying 'Follow, follow!' crashed off through low scrub and left us.

'Follow, follow!' said Anna frantically. She flapped her hands at us, stolidly chewing away. 'You follow their tracking signs,' she cried. 'Circles and arrows and go back to base, and so on. Come *on*!'

We clambered up and glumly trotted after her. We trotted for ages. Then Anna dropped to her knees.

'An arrow!' she cried. We strained our eyes. A bit of old bent gorse lay on the ground. 'There!' said Anna, pointing dramatically to the horizon like King Arthur pointing out further glories in the sky to his knights. 'Kom.'

We followed like fools – right into the middle of the biggest, oldest, most savage gorse thicket that I had ever seen. We sat in complete silence, Cherry still clutching the Nature Collection Tobacco Tin. I noticed that she had managed to tie her skirt sideways, sarong-style, like Dorothy Lamour.

'You cold?' demanded Anna. But Cherry was too indignant to answer.

There was a distant shout and I looked up. Then I stiffened with delight. Through a gap in the gorse patch we could see strange country stretching away. In front of us was long dry grass waving gently on flat ground, wind-bent trees and water. Reeds moved this way and that in the glittering light.

I sank down in peace in that real land. Not in a peasant's hut would I live, I decided, but in a bare wooden house with polished floors, and rooms big enough to let the wind in. As a faded aristocrat, I would salvage one cut-glass chandelier from the ruin of my estate. I would light it at night, and watch its crystal spears of light pierce, not Europe's snow falling outside my windows, but

the brief shadows of those wind-bent trees, that whispering grass,
the black reeds moving soundlessly in my stretch of water.
 Waiting for the swans to fly in from Denmark.

The Swans

'Arms folded, dears,' said Miss Martin in her special getting-ready-to-read-*Milly-Molly-Mandy* voice. 'Now, let me see,' she said, peering at the book. 'Why, goodness me, here is a picture of a jam pot.' She held the book up and we all fastened our eyes on that pot of jam drawn beside the firm black print.

'Now what is Milly-Molly-Mandy doing with a jam pot?'

Cherry and I turned our heads and our eyes flew together like magnet and iron. Here was another detail of our Old Age Plan to note down. When we were old, old women, we were going to both settle down in a nice white cottage with a thatched roof, like Milly-Molly-Mandy's, in the main street of the settlement. We were going to sweep and dust and arrange our cottage-garden flowers in pottery bowls and make cups of tea for visitors.

Every day we added another little detail to the Old Age Plan.

'A chair for *me*,' Cherry would chant, 'and a chair for *you*, Astrid. And every morning and every night we are going to feed our hens and ducks. Won't it be nice, Astrid? Won't it be nice?'

'Yes, oh yes!' I would say. 'And every morning and every night we will ask the hens and the ducks and swans what the next day's weather is to be, and they will tell us!'

And every time I said that, or talked about birds or animals speaking to us, Cherry turned a deep, offended pink.

'That's not *true*, Astrid!' she would cry. 'You just make all that stuff up like your Grandmother. You know birds can't speak! We will just feed our hens, Astrid, with pollard in the morning, and wheat at night. And they will lay eggs for our tea. And that's all.'

There was a fence growing between us. I tried to tell her of 'The Wild Swans', by H. C. Andersen, but she would not listen. Swans spoke in that story, as they did in lots of Danish stories.

Tante Helga read to Anna Friis and me in a holy voice.

> When the sun began to slide down behind the sea, Elsa saw eleven wild swans, with golden crowns on their heads, flying towards the beach. Like a white ribbon being pulled across the sky, they flew one after the other . . .

In that story, as in lots of Danish stories, there was a sacred woman, sometimes young and beautiful, sometimes bent and old. She always knew what was going to happen. She knew the language of the birds of Denmark.

My Bedstemoder's eyes changed when she heard Tante Helga read. She regarded us steadily, chin sunk into one hand.

'Girls change into swans, in Denmark,' she said. 'And young princes sometimes. In Denmark, at certain times of the year, the swans speak to us.'

'Who hears them?' I asked, knowing the answer.

'Certain men,' said my Bedstemoder, 'and certain women.' And not another word would she say.

I worried that we had left Denmark behind. We had left behind those wise men and women. But H. C. Andersen knew about us. In the middle of 'The Wild Swans' he had written about the seas that circled us far away in New Zealand.

> When the clouds above it are dark, then the sea becomes as black as they are, and yet it will put on a dress of white if the wind should suddenly come and whip the waves. . . .

Elsa's broders were turned into swans. They could only cross the ocean if they found a rock to stand on when the sun set, when they were changed back into men. But *I* thought the seas we have sailed across, in our swan-winged ships, are too big for us. We will lose our voices, we will lose ourselves. We will never see the swans from Denmark again. There will be no more wise Danish women to teach us the secrets of life.

One Saturday we went on an expedition, Anna, Cherry and I. We were just discovering the far countries that lay beyond our farms. We wanted to see what lay behind the low hill at the back of Barrett's farm. Anything might be there, said Anna and I to Cherry. On our expedition we took the Nature Notebooks, pencils, tobacco tins, sandwiches and a great vinegar jar of lemon juice.

Cherry didn't really like big expeditions. She liked the equipment we took, the Nature Notebooks and the collecting tins for Miss Martin, and the lunch. But she didn't like the bush or the creek.

'Spooky places!' she would cry, and stay rooted like a stone. 'Don't go in there, Astrid!' she would plead. 'Astrid?' But I always followed Anna.

That Saturday we went through strange farmers' paddocks. One of them shouted at us as we mooned through the grass. Cherry hid in a haystack and shook. She would not come out, so Anna Friis crawled into her sanctuary.

'You want the lemon juice – and lunch?' asked Anna Friis casually.

'Yes, oh yes!' cried Cherry, and hastily crawled out, hay all over her. We brushed her down, then started our climb. We climbed to the top of the hill, lugging our equipment. Waves of gold grass ran over our feet, whispered words into our ears, and raced on to the edge of the world.

Anna Friis turned wild. She raced the grass-waves, calling out, 'Here I will live for ever, for ever! For ever and ever and ever!'

Then Cherry and I saw it. There was a *lake* behind that hill. Blue water, green raupos. We both stared, our mouths open. But Anna tore down the hill, hanging on to the lemon-drink jar.

'Don't you spill our lemon drink, Anna Friis!' shouted Cherry suddenly, turning red and indignant. She turned to me. 'We will have nothing to drink.'

'We will drink of the waters of that lake,' I said poetically.

We set off through the restless grass. At the lake edge I stood and looked into its clear water. Snails were under the surface, travelling their grass-stem highways. In a flash, Cherry Taylor was crouched down, opening her tobacco tin, busily talking to those snails.

'Snailies, little snailies,' she droned, 'come into your nice new house.' She scooped her tin under the water. The snails were reluctant to be welcomed into their new home. Then I looked up. Anna Friis had stopped, and in front of her, not far from the lake edge, was a small house. An old, clean, white, wooden house. In front of its porch was a stretch of freshly washed concrete, white as milk. From the chimney at the back rose the smoke from its hearth fire. And, sitting on a kitchen chair on the edge of the white concrete was an old, old woman. Anna jerked her head at me. Slowly, very slowly, I walked towards her. Behind us, Cherry stopped dead.

'*No*, Astrid,' she said. This was the same as the bush, as the creek. But I went on. We stopped on the grass in front of that white concrete and did our bobs.

'Good morning.' I said in Miss Martin's social voice.

'Goddag,' said the old woman.

Then, 'Goddag,' said Anna in her Moder's cold, dark voice. 'Hvordan har du det?'

'Godt, tak,' said the old woman. 'Og du?'

'Godt, tak,' said Anna.

'Godt, tak,' I said.

The old woman sat and looked steadily at us. Her eyes were as blue and as clear as glass, as the lake-water. She wore a dark-blue handkerchief knotted behind, and her clean white apron, now that the morning's work was done. Ready for guests.

'What are you doing?' asked Anna in Danish.

'Looking at the world. Looking for what I will see,' answered the old woman. Her Danish was very harsh and guttural. South Jutland Danish. *Our* part of the country.

'What will you see?' asked Anna.

'This and that. Secrets of men,' said the old woman. She held out a hand to Anna. 'Kom,' she commanded. Anna moved and took the hand.

'Danish child,' said the old woman, 'dearest child.' And, one-two, she kissed Anna on both cheeks, in the old way of greeting. And Anna curtsied in the old way. Then, 'Farvel,' said the old woman. 'Farvel, barn.'

'Don't you drop that lemon drink!' shouted Cherry Taylor, from her safe distance. Then she screamed.

Drifting into open water, feathers stained faintly with mud, *dangerous*, were three white swans. Their black eyes took us in. Then the long necks turned indifferently, wearily away; the strong feet pulled against the water. The swans glided towards the edge of the lake to where that house was. The old woman was leaning forward.

'Kom, kom, mine darlings!' she called.

'Who is she?' I whispered in our dream to Anna.

'Valborg Hansen,' answered Anna in our dream. 'She lives alone since her husband die. She will not go to her datter's hus in Longburn. My Mor told me.'

At a safe distance along the lake Cherry was down on the grass, laying out the lunch. We slowly walked towards her.

'My word,' chattered Cherry Taylor, 'that mad old woman *did* give me a fright! Fancy living in that crazy house alone, beside a creepy lake.'

She suddenly looked up, and fell silent. No more Milly-Molly-Mandy in thatched cottages in our old age. No more roses or cups of tea. Two wise women of South Jutland looked at her from their cold eyes. Anna and Astrid, living in a plain white wooden house, when their husbands were gone.

Living by water, talking to swans stained by long travel.

Hearing the latest news from Denmark.

The School Picnic

Do you know Foxton?

Ah well – that is where we had the school picnics. When you say that name, 'Foxton', I see blue and white and silver. The waves were big there, you see, pounding in from the ocean, breaking and breaking on the bar of the river. Birds whirled above the water and the sand-hills flashed their silver grains in the sun.

I ran and shouted over miles of that hard river sand, when I could first run.

My Fader and my Moder told me of the Danish beach houses which once were there, and our beach house, its name 'Vegas' painted on a wooden shield on its front wall, where the burning sand drifted in heaps, whirling in front of the great gales that blew in from over the ocean. They had a boat, called *The Viking*. My Bedstefader took all his family out, each morning, dressed in their bathing-suits. He paused by the edge of the roaring sea.

'Regard,' he would cry, morning after morning, 'the wondrous ocean!' Then he would put his hands together in the attitude of prayer, and puffing out his cheeks he would dive, splish-splash, through the nearest wave. And his family followed, like leaping dolphins.

My Mor told me how, in the afternoons, the screaming sea birds floated down to earth and stood, facing the ocean over the bar, and lifted their wings in the shining light of the wet river sand where the tide had ebbed. Then the Danish families promenaded, in straw hats with flowers and white dresses for the women, and hats with wide brims and flowing cravats and white linen suits for the men.

The School Picnic

They walked up and down the wide hard sands of the river flats prodding shells and ribbons of seaweed with their canes, with the silver knobs, with the black jet knobs. And one summer, Onkel Sigurd fell in love with an English girl. My Moder said that they went for long walks, and spoke poetry to each other. And she called him – 'My Tolstoi'. And he called her – 'My Titania'.

I could always see them in the long gentle summer afternoons, walking farther and farther away, in a flutter of white muslin and linen, until they dwindled and vanished in the heat haze that danced over the white sandhills.

But my Bedstemoder told me another story.

On that river bar, she said, out of the sea mist one morning, came the black masts of a ship from Denmark. Bedstefar stood on its deck. It was a fast ship, she said, built like the old long-ships, and it cut through the water like a knife. It had a golden figurehead of a mer-maiden, a child of the sea, and when the ship came to rest at Foxton, the long slanting eyes of that mer-child looked blindly at the new land. And I saw our Danish people land and stand in their long black travelling cloaks, looking through their slanting dark blue eyes at the new land. Sea travellers for a thousand years, this was the farthest land they had reached.

All these stories I remembered on the day of the school picnic, on the day I was King of the French Cricket. And that was the only day I was King. My eye was in, and every ball that came, I hit. The Headmaster, wearing a shameful old straw hat, sat bolt upright on a campstool with his whistle around his neck. Around his feet lounged his throne followers, those boys who vowed to become Headmasters, and wear spectacles and whistles around their necks, and hold Assemblies. I could hear their talk from where I stood, firmly holding my tennis racket, guarding my knees, defending my one-day reign as King of the French Cricket.

'Please, Sir, is it true, Sir,' came an obsequious voice thinned out by the sea wind. 'that the tide rises and falls in obedience to the waxing and waning of the moon?'

The thrower of the ball pulled a hideous face at me, spat on his hands and ran like a hurricane. I hit the ball.

'Up the huzzars!' yelled my Fader, from a nearby sand mound. 'How's *that*, Sir?'

The Bear from the North

Behind me the Headmaster's voice droned on: 'The tides, Flemmington, rise and fall . . .'

Then we had the races.

The little ones lined up first. They ran slowly, looking back at their Moders, who could not contain their anxiety and ran beside them, their flowered crepe-de-chine dresses fluttering against their legs, holding their hats on sideways with one hand, and laughing.

Then it was our turn. I was going to emulate my Onkel Sven, who had won the New Zealand Mile. I crouched like Sven and was off like a rabbit. But I could not catch up with Cherry Taylor, who had limbs made of leather. I came limping back to my family and collapsed on the sand, breathing like a traction engine. But my Fader was away in his stories of Sven's great Training Programme.

'We never knew he was Preparing,' he said to the Lessingtons, who sat beside us on the soft fringed travelling rugs where we all sat. 'Day after day, in the back paddock, there was good old Sven, puffing round and round like the Foxton Flyer.' Here Far gave his great puffs like the Foxton Flyer, working his arms to suggest the railway wheels in motion. 'And his only audience was his old cat. She runs with him and when she gets puffed, up she hops on to a fence post and waits to get her breath back, while old Sven, he charges around the paddock once more to get his legs into training.'

Tears came into Far's eyes as usual, as he saw Sven again, winning the New Zealand Mile. 'Limbs like the wind,' he said for the hundredth time. 'He brings us home a biscuit barrel and a silver cup with his name on it.'

And for the hundredth time Mr Lessington looked down his nose for such lack of modesty in Fader's words.

Last of all, the big boys ran their race. And it was a different race to ours. Nobody laughed, nobody called out loving messages. The mothers sat silent, and the fathers leaned forward and gave strange savage roars. The boys ran round and round the track marked in the sand, their faces twisted with their agony to win. And Mr Prebble, who helped run all the races down in the dark sunken Recreation Ground, at home, crouched in his best suit and hat and rang a big bell when they had nearly finished and cried something to them in

The School Picnic

a strange wailing language, which Fader said was 'One Lap to Go, Boys! One Lap to Go!' and when it was over some boys collapsed on the sand and rolled around groaning.

'You'd think running is a battle,' said Far. 'That old Sven now – all he does is spit on the ground and give his great laugh. He does not care if he win or not. He likes only to run.'

Mr Lessington glared silently out towards the ocean.

Miss Martin blew her whistle.

'Come, come, little ones!' she called. She had Arthur Mee in her hands.

We sighed in our straggling wind-blown line in front of her. For how could Arthur Mee make his voice heard here, under the great brass cymbal of that sun, against the savage roar of those waves out on the bar?

'Sea wrack, winkles and sea lavender,' read Miss Martin with some difficulty, as Arthur Mee helplessly fluttered his pages in the wind. 'Come, come!' called Miss Martin. 'Fan out. Find the treasures of the sea.'

We fanned out, and glumly clumped along, looking for treasures of the sea. We found pipi shells, some seaweed and one old bottle.

'*Well*,' said Miss Martin when we laid our treasures at her feet, 'we have only begun! This afternoon we will seek *and* find.'

Faintly in the distance a whistle blew. Gaunt against the pine trees stood the Headmaster, summoning us to lunch. We ran like wolves.

'*Some* people,' said Miss Gore, tight-lipped, pouring free orange fizz into cups, 'have manners and do not rush like animals to their food.'

We sipped daintily, little fingers stuck out, to show that we were not animals, rushing rudely to our dinners. Watching us were the big gentle mothers in their drooping beach hats.

'More?' they asked, and tenderly watched us, their little lambs, as we drank it all down. Georgie Manners had six cups. My Bedstemoder watched him keenly.

'You will overflow,' she said to him calmly. Georgie Manners belched, and then drooped before Miss Gore's outraged eye.

We sat in groups on the travelling rugs and ate our lunch. The river glittered, the seagulls cried, and above my head, the adults remembered other days.

'Over there,' said my Bedstefader, sweeping his arm, 'was the old wharf. There the ship holding the Scandinavians came to rest. Flags were put out by the English. The barracks were over there. Our people spent the whole night singing and dancing.'

But my Bedstemoder looked at the dancing river, and the land stretching back that we had drained and farmed.

'I remember,' she said, 'I remember just now the young Danes. The young men who had never cut down trees. I remember their bleeding hands, and my Moder and us girls bandaging them. I remember the fires that burned night and day, killing the bush. The Day of Judgement.'

'Ah, my Abild,' said my Bedstefader, touching her hand, 'those were the old days. Look now at the river, at the children. Think of all the great things that were done by the Danes.'

But my Bedstemoder could not stop.

'My sister,' she said, 'lille Marie. Do you remember how she went so far through the bush after the fires, to see how her friend Anna Sorensen was, and Anna had had her child and died? And Anna's husband was distraught with his grief. And we looked up from our Middag, and there was Marie standing at the door with the child in her arms. And she said, "This is the child of my friend Anna Sorensen, and we have killed the land with the fires, and Anna has died for what we have done." And you know what happened to Marie. You know! She died so young, worn out with work. So young.'

'Kom,' said my Moder. She took my hand, sticky with the free orange fizz, and led me down to the wet sand beside the river. 'She is remembering some sad things today. The river has reminded her of the old days.'

We stood in the long afternoon light.

'Now,' said my Mor, 'one summer here your Grandonkel Sigurd fell in love with an English girl. She called him "My Tolstoi" and he called her "My Titania".'

Over the river the seagulls wailed, over the water where the ship from Denmark had come to rest at last, flying its long scarlet streamers, the dragon's-breath, to salute the new land.

The Old Ones

In the Spring, in the Manawatu, the gales blow – the grass runs and turns dark-green, and then silver as the high clouds race across the sky. One moment, the land looks itself – but the next moment, it turns into something else entirely. The wind swoops over the flax-blades on the river bank. They flicker their long swords, they clack their long tongues, gossiping of the old times. Then the sky seems to darken, the prows of the long war canoes knife through the water and the chants of the warriors echo up the river bank to where the huts of the first settlers stood in the mud. The first huts of the English and the Dane.

One Spring day, I found the book. It was in that cupboard in the living room with the glass doors. I opened the book and there they were: the silver people. They were in a picture, a close-up of a silver bowl. All around the bowl were decorations. I tilted the book to see, and the figures suddenly shone out in the strong light. One figure was a man sleeping on the ground, with a plaited garland for the spring around his neck. One was a man standing up, and facing him was a woman, holding out a garland for him too. Over their heads flew a bird. I looked at the man standing up. He was looking at the woman with the branch. I could just see the expression on his face. He was half smiling. And so was she. As if they knew something. Secrets. Underneath the picture ran heavy black old-fashioned Danish print. 'Details of silver bowl found in Jutland peat bog. The figures are said to be a representation of the spring . . .'

A hand came down on that book, covering it as the hawk covers

The Bear from the North

its prey. I gasped and looked up. My Bedstemoder said, 'You leave those old people alone!'

I looked at her, and you know, her face had changed. It was fierce, it was guarding something.

'Who are those people?' I asked her. She looked at me, and then she looked at the picture. Her face went still again. I did not know her.

'They died many years ago, but the faces are the same,' she said.

'But what are they *doing*?'

She looked at me, but did not see me.

'They brought the spring,' she said abruptly, 'to Jutland.'

Then she regretted saying that. She became angry.

'Go *out*side,' she said to me. '*Out*side!' and banged the book shut.

So I went outside into the spring gales. Something in that picture, something in that wind, made me run. I ran and shouted through the thrashing grass. I ran and leapt and shouted words that no man knew any more.

That night when we had dinner, I watched my Bedstemoder, I watched my Moder. While we ate our dinner, they slanted their eyes away from time to time, over our heads, out of the windows. What did they see? Their eyes took on a coldness, a remoteness. They looked into the dark world outside. What children of the dead did they see? What ghosts of Jutland warriors, what queens and kings with their silver hoards? For we brought our ghosts with us over the seas between New Zealand and Denmark. They cast their long-armed shadows over the Manawatu Plains. I craned to see the sky outside the window. All I saw were faint pin-pricks of light. Stars. Jewels glittering in a dead king's crown.

On the Monday after, I took my basket to school for the daffodils. For the Daffodil Day.

'See how many daffodils people will give you,' said Miss Martin. 'We want plenty for our stall in the settlement tomorrow.' For that was what we did. We sold the daffodils tied up in little bunches, for money for our school. Money for books, money for things for the school. That was my first Daffodil Day. It was so strange, when we should have been indoors doing the Spelling, doing the Arithmetic, to bike along the roads, looking for the farmlands where the daffodils grew. The first and oldest farms in the district, where people had planted daffodils a long time ago, so that now they had spread, right over the Spring paddocks. We went in groups of four. My group was Anna Friis, her brother Kjeld, Rangi Katene and me. We biked along the road where the farms with the oldest gardens were. The first and oldest farms in the district where the people had planted daffodils a long time ago.

Well, the wind blew, the grass on the Plains turned green and silver, and stretches of floodwater in the paddocks flashed like knives as the sun caught them.

Anna and I raced our bikes into the wind, but Kjeld and Rangi were older and they rode more slowly, looking seriously for daffodils. At least, Rangi did, but that Kjeld, Anna's broder, he biked in a dream, twisting his front wheel this way and that. And every time I looked back he seemed to be watching me, but how could you tell? His eyes were long and slanting, as they watched, but his mouth half-smiled, thinking of some secret. It was a secret I did not know, and I needed to. Oh yes. I liked that smile; his lovely secret.

Rangi was shy, but she kept her eyes sharp, looking for the daffodils. Suddenly she stopped, and stood in the gravel road. She pointed to a house, far away from the road. You could see the chimneys sticking out of the pine shelter-belt.

'Daffodils here,' she said.

We circled back, Anna and I.

'Oh, Rangi!' I shouted all puffed up to be with senior people. 'Will they let us pick them for our school?'

'There are plenty,' said Rangi. 'We came here last year. I know this place. It used to be Maori land. You come with me now.'

The gate was of two big posts made of stone. One had a ball on the top. The ball from the other post had fallen down. Periwinkle was growing over it, so I knew that that house was very old. My Moder had told me that. The periwinkle knows houses that are very old, and grows there, my Mor said. We wheeled our bikes up the drive. Old pine trees spread out on either side. They had hard green moss on the sides of their trunks that didn't get the sun. We turned a corner and there were the daffodils. Hundreds of them.

The Bear from the North

My fingers itched to snap their juicy stems, but Rangi kept on to the house. I looked back to see if Kjeld liked the daffodils too, but he was just drifting along with his basket bumping on the handle-bars, gazing at the trees, at the daffodils, still with that half-smile. He did not look at us. Was he a fool, a simple boy? Why did he smile like that all the time?

But Rangi was propping her bike against the last tree. I laid my bike carefully down in the grass. Then I saw the house. Ah now, that was a really old house. The veranda was so old that part of it had been taken down, so that some of the doors were straight above the ground. And at the back of the house stood a piece of very old bush. They say that the Plains were covered with bush like that, before the white people came. That bush would have seen Maori canoes slipping down the muddy river long ago. My skin prickled, but Rangi went straight up to one of those doors so high above the ground and knocked.

Nobody came. We stood and looked at each other.

'The teacher said this was one of the houses that gives us flowers,' said Anna. 'This is the house of Mrs Somerset-White.' Her voice sounded very harsh.

'You mean we just go ahead and *pick*?' I said.

'Sh-sh,' said Rangi, and she looked at that house.

'These people know us,' said Rangi, as if she knew it by heart.

Anna pressed her lips together and knocked again. Still nobody came. Kjeld came out of his dream.

'More daffodils than anywhere else here,' he said. He picked up his basket and waded into the grass. And we started to pick. Oh yes. I have never picked so many daffodils since in my life. The juice from the stalks ran down my fingers. And as I picked, I noticed their centres. Not lemon-yellow, but deep red. That made me stop. That, and their smell. Very sweet. Too sweet. It filled your body and made the head swim.

Just as I stopped picking, one of the doors in the house opened and standing on a faded carpet was an old, old woman. She was peeling an apple and little bits of apple skin clung to her woollen dress. She was so old that she did not notice. She looked at us, and then she saw Rangi. She smiled then, and spoke. I could not understand, and then I did. That old woman, her family had come so long ago from England, but she spoke to Rangi in Maori. And Rangi spoke back. We stood and smiled, but she spoke only to Rangi. Then she shut the door. Rangi turned and walked away, and we followed, struggling with our flower-baskets and the bikes.

'What did she say, Rangi?' we asked over and over. But Rangi only said, 'We can have the daffodils. She knows us. The Maoris know her. And she knows our people. You know what she said to me? She said, it should be flax-flowers you are picking. Flax-flowers for the spring!' She laughed.

We had a hard job getting home, against that wind. Rangi turned in at her gate, and we pedalled on, straining to keep the bikes moving. Anna and Kjeld were to leave their daffodils in our washhouse tubs, and Far was taking them to school the next day. As we turned in at our gate, my Bedstemoder was standing on the veranda. She held out her hands in greeting to us – and to our daffodils.

Kjeld came up behind us. He let his bike drop and went up the steps to my Bedstemoder. I watched him. His eyes slanted against the strong spring light, and as he held up the basket to my Bedstemoder, his lips curled in that half-smile, that dream, that secret. She leaned forward and took his flowers. Then she smiled that half-smile back at him, her lips curving down too, over their secret.

The wind roared in my ears, and dropped away into silence. The air touched my skin with a cold finger. Then I shivered.

Not with the wind.

Not with the air.

But with the memory of that silver bowl, the people on it, buried so long ago in a Jutland peat bog. The woman, the priestess, holding out the branch of flowers, the young warrior facing her, and on the ground, already gone to fetch the spring, the other young warrior, smiling at his fate, with the plaited noose around his neck.

My Bedstemoder spoke to Kjeld. Two words.

'Dansk Mand.'

Danish Man.

Then she buried her face deep into the daffodils as if she could never have enough of them. The strange daffodils with the red centres. Red as men's blood.

Armistice Day

From the nursery warmth of Miss Martin's infant room, tender as young geraniums flowering behind glass, we spied on the senior school. In the mornings there was an austere silence about that red-brick building. Sometimes a figure of a big boy or girl sped out of a door and marched, frowning responsibly, in the direction of the school toilets hidden behind the macrocarpa hedge. After a discreet interval, they marched back again. Sometimes a dull roar came out of the windows of Standard Five and Six.

> '*Twice* twelve are twenty-four,
> *Thrice* twelve are thirty-six!'

Thrice! We marvelled at that word.
And we heard –
'*London* is the capital of England! King George the *Fifth* is the King of Great Britain . . .'
They were terribly keen on kings in that building. And on war.
In the afternoons we watched the seniors at their war games. They came out in a long black line, swinging their arms, scowling, and marched all over the tennis court. By the flag pole stood the Headmaster, waiting for the lines to come to a dead stop in front of him. Miss Martin's children anxiously sucked their thumbs at the sight of that Headmaster. He was coloured grey – grey suit, grey face, grey hair and grey teeth. We hid behind bushes when we saw him coming, pointing imperiously. We watched the senior children darting about, stuffing paper bags into rubbish tins, or

Armistice Day

tearing out weeds with dreadful obsequious smiles. When we came face to face with him, we skittered past like ghosts, with our eyes half closed, so that he could not see us.

Our room was different from the rest of that school. It was always a sea of paste, newspaper, raffia, infant scissors, paste-encrusted brushes and plasticine. And our room was swayed by the latest ideas from the *Teachers' Monthly Guide*. It came all the way from England to be collected by Miss Martin from the Fancy Goods and Stationery Shop in the settlement. We clustered around her when she opened it, and gazed at those British girls and boys, calm, pale, *clever*, in their orderly classrooms, beside their Projects. Once they had made a model English village – out of what seemed to be cardboard and pieces of straw. We made one too. I became an authority on the Old English thatched cottage. We ranged tirelessly over other people's gardens, seeking good bits of moss for the Old English crazy paving paths that went with all those cottages. All my life since, I have not been able to pass a good crop of moss without a twitch in my fingers.

But one Monday we were faced by Miss Martin, cheeks pink with anxiety.

'Who has straight backs?' asked Miss Martin. 'Who can keep in step?' We gazed hopelessly at her. 'Today,' cried poor Miss Martin, 'we are going to join in with Assembly! Isn't that lovely now?'

It wasn't. With drooping mouths we waited for the signal. It came. A death-rattle on the school drum.

'Heads up!' pleaded Miss Martin, and we stuck out our chests and stumbled out of our door, cardigans around our elbows, hair hanging over our eyes, under the jeering gaze of the rest of the school, drawn up in their fearful ranks.

The Headmaster tapped one foot as we shuffled into place.

'Raise the right hand!' he commanded. Miss Martin's class became confused. Some raised the right hand, some the left, but most of us, knowing we were about to die, raised both.

'Boy!' growled the Headmaster. The drummer boy glared over our heads and started another death-rattle.

'I *love* God and my country,' warned the Headmaster. Ah! The poetry speaking! Miss Martin's class loved poetry speaking.

'I *love* God and my country!' we piped, beaming.
'I will honour the flag!'
'I will honour the flag!'
'And honour the King!'
'And honour the King!'
'And cheerfully obey the laws of the land . . .'
'And cheerfully –'

But I was far away, peering at the far end of the playground, to where I distinctly saw the sad figure of King George the Fifth on his horse, saluting us, in what appeared to be a snowstorm, just outside Moscow.

Back in the classroom, Miss Martin gave her little announcement. 'Soon, my dears, is Armistice Day, and you are going to march all the way down the road, with the whole school, and put lovely flowers on the War Memorial. Today was just a practice, and you looked beautiful!'

We didn't believe it. Neither did Miss Martin. Her cheeks were flushed again. We should have taken that as a warning. 'I have had an idea,' announced Miss Martin, and she held up a giant picture in the *Teachers' Monthly Guide*. There those British children stood, proud but calm, dressed in suits of armour and lovely helmets, apparently made from cardboard boxes and little bits of chocolate paper. 'We,' said Miss Martin simply, 'are going to make helmets for our Armistice Day march.' Who could resist those helmets, the plumes, and so on? 'Feathers,' cried Miss Martin, becoming dangerously excited, 'and cardboard! You will have to *scour* the district!'

We commenced the scouring.

At home, I gave the family the news.

'On Armistice Day,' I announced at dinner, 'we are going to be old-fashioned soldiers of the British Empire.'

The family looked *amazed*.

'Warriors!' said my Bedstemoder, in a voice that should have warned me. 'Ha!' She spent the evening searching through the bookcase. She gave me a vast red book with a piece of paper sticking out of it. On the paper was carefully printed, 'Dansk

Armistice Day

Warrior of Old Days.'

I bore it to school.

Miss Martin excitedly opened it. There stood a Viking warrior wearing his fearsome helmet with the horns on. She peeped at him. The Viking glowered at Miss Martin. Miss Martin smartly shut the book.

'*Horns*, Astrid,' she said, 'would be a little hard to *find*!'

'We have some horns!' said Betty Cooper. 'Old cows' horns that Dad –'

'*British* soldiers,' said Miss Martin, 'did not wear horns. Perhaps one day we will have a parade of warriors of the world. But just for now – feathers – and cardboard!'

I haunted the henyard, eyeing the hens, and I haunted the local store, gazing hungrily at a cardboard sign of a lovely lady in a picture hat. 'Smoke Desert Gold,' announced the lady. I wished to see the other side of her, to see if the cardboard was snowy white. *Usable*.

'Taking up smoking now, are we?' asked the store keeper, and hooted at his joke, day after day.

The days sped by to Armistice Day. Miss Martin grew haggard with the surprise. We did the sums, the compositions, with our eyes flickering regularly to those intricate cardboard shapes trailing long pieces of tape hanging from nails on the walls.

Outside, long lines of children marched to the drum beat, the Headmaster barked commands, practising.

On the afternoon before the great day, Betty Cooper ventured to clear up a little mystery.

'Miss Martin,' she said, 'What is Armistice Day for?'

'Well –' began Miss Martin all over again, 'at the stroke of eleven, all over the Empire, everybody stops whatever he or she is doing – and Remembers . . .'

But while she talked, we glanced out of the window. And there, on the tennis court, sat a line of senior girls, twisting pieces of macrocarpa into wheels. We peered more intently. The macrocarpa wheels were wreaths, the kind you sent to funerals.

On the Day, we assembled early. Too early. We rushed to meet Miss Martin as she came to unlock the classroom door. Miss Martin

The Bear from the North

checked when she saw us – best purses embroidered with raffia daisies, patent-leather shoes, best dresses with the fullness.

'Now remember,' she said 'we must keep *up*, and not dawdle. We must be assembled in plenty of time for the speeches, for the wreath-laying, so that at eleven o'clock precisely, we may observe the *Silence*.'

We did the Arithmetic, to calm the nerves. Then the school bell tolled for the dead, as usual; only this day, with more significance. With trembling fingers, we put on our helmets. I had harvested a fine collection of feathers for mine. It would ruffle nobly in a light breeze, I had thought. Through a storm of feathers in the rising wind, I watched with the others as the columns set off, to the battle drum-roll from that boy in Standard Six. We stayed somewhat concealed behind the school hedge.

'We do not wish to reveal our surprise too early!' explained Miss Martin.

Last of all the classes, we set off. But fate was against us. The road was covered with gravel; our patent-leather best shoes felt every stone. Our purses got in the way when we swung our arms. Then from far behind us we heard the remorseless tread of marching feet coming nearer and nearer. Peering through my feathers, I saw the Scout Troop, led by Mr Prowse, the Scout Leader. Behind him big boys held banners. Those banners were so pretty.

'March just a little faster, dears!' urged Miss Martin.

Our helmets started to slip. My eyes were slowly covered in darkness. By peering intently through one side of my eye-piece, I saw Cherry Taylor, wearing her rustling flower-girl-dress, go slowly and more slowly.

With a fine flurry of flags and drums the Scout Troop shouldered past. I distinctly heard Mr Prowse ask what the hell did we think we were doing, dressed up like sore toes and painted savages. We ignored him.

'Push up your helmets, dears,' urged Miss Martin.

We hung on to our helmets and purses with one arm and swung the other.

Far down the road, a sombre crowd clustered around the War Memorial. We faintly heard the drums.

Armistice Day

'*Faster*, dears!' said Miss Martin, low but urgent. 'Swing your arms!' We swung our arms. Our helmets commenced the slipping again. Miss Martin fell back to retrieve Cherry Taylor, who had tripped.

We marched on, past the first houses of the settlement, past the iron ranks of the senior warriors, past the Headmaster, standing in helpless rage among his funeral wreaths by the granite War Memorial, he and it the same grey. And helmets muffling our proud smiles, heedless of Miss Martin's warning cries, we marched on and on, and came to a halt at last, far, far past the War Memorial. Then, feathers in our mouths, we saw the incredulous faces of that silent crowd of parents, mine among them, and I heard, I *heard* the shameful, uncontrollable laughter of Onkel Sven echo over the ruins of Armistice Day.

Who laughed with him? The Fallen. Our Dead.

I think they get so tired of all those bugles and drums. I think they loved our helmets.

Coronation Day

In 1937 Cherry Taylor and I turned into Princess Elizabeth and Princess Margaret Rose. It was the Coronation that did it. And that beautiful book *Our Princesses and Their Dogs* that Onkel Sven had bought me for my birthday.

Oh, the photographs in that book! They were in sepia, exactly the same colour as the mushrooms in our cow paddock. Cherry and I knew all the stories under the photographs by heart.

'Come along!' calls Princess Elizabeth, across the south lawn at Royal Lodge. 'Time for dinner!'

And there was Princess Elizabeth, not wearing the crown or the ermine, but a simple maidenly dress, holding out a royal dog dish to an army of corgis battle-charging across a closely mown paddock to their dinner.

'There won't be enough dinner for all those dogs,' mourned Cherry, peering at the one meagre royal dog dish. But I was concentrating on Princess Elizabeth's simple maidenly dress.

'She's wearing my dirndl,' I said, 'but with terrible great shoes.'

'*Not* terrible great shoes, Astrid,' said Cherry, in an earnest teacher's voice that set my teeth on edge. 'They have to wear strong shoes to get themselves all over the sweeping lawns.'

'I have a dirndl,' I said.

The blouse for my dirndl was a bit too bright for the simple dignity of the princesses. It had the embroideries of the wheat-ears and the cornflowers of Denmark, and blue wavy lines for the waters of the Baltic and the North Sea. We looked doubtfully at the simple blouses of the princesses. Cherry read in a reverent voice:

> Two simple little English girls at play on a summer's day. The Princess Elizabeth and Margaret Rose show the Duke and Duchess of York how obedient their doggies are!

We gazed spellbound at the doggies, all sitting up and begging – except for one, who was slinking away into the furtive shade of a giant rhododendron. A nurse with a veil was bolting after him.

'That's Dandy,' said Cherry in an indulgent voice. 'He's a dag that one, always running away . . .'

'Are they living in a hospital?' I asked, gazing at the bolting nurse.

'That's Allah!' cried Cherry, shocked at my ignorance. 'She's their nurse.'

'Are they sick?' I insisted.

'Not a nurse. A nanny,' said Cherry deeply. Ah.

And day after day we turned into the princesses. Me in my dirndl with the vulgar embroideries, and Cherry in a dirndl made from one of my cardigans lashed together with a long brown bootlace, a very simple blouse and a skirt. We both wore our heaviest lace-up shoes with the white socks. Then we clumped up and down the south lawn of Royal Lodge, calling now and then to the corgi-horde, or waving in a lady-like way to the crowds outside the royal garden walls.

'They are locked away from the crowds,' explained Cherry, 'for they are special people.'

'Locked away?'

Cherry looked pityingly at this Danish dolt.

'Now we will take the photographs, Astrid,' she said. We peered at our favourite photograph. Underneath it the story said,

> 'Sit up Dandy!' says the Princess Elizabeth.

'There's good old Dandy,' we said to each other. Dandy was not only sitting up – he had lain his ears ecstatically against the Princess

The Bear from the North

Elizabeth's royal chin. That dog knew where his dinner came from, I thought, but did not dare say so aloud.

'We will have to use your dog,' said Cherry firmly.

Bor the fox-terrier peered warily at us from underneath our wash house. We hauled him out by one leg.

'Now go on,' urged Cherry, 'you are Princess Elizabeth, Astrid.' Heavens! I hung on to struggling Bor and lowered my chin winningly on top of his ears. Bor gave my face his usual loving lick but, as Heir to the Throne, I did not flinch. Cherry raised her imaginary camera. She chanted slowly and reverently, ' "Sit up Dandy!" says the Princess Elizabeth . . . Click.'

Then we did the next bit. We had not been able to gather much information about what the princesses actually did, but careful research in endless newspaper photographs revealed their other occupation. They walked, outside those garden walls, from great black cars into large public buildings. Stooping modestly, they peeped at the crowds from under large felt hats, with simple buttoned coats, long socks, buttoned shoes and hands in gloves.

We gazed thoughtfully at each other and went to work on our bewildered Moders. And so we got our new winter outfits – the large felt hats, the simple coats, the long socks and the buttoned shoes.

We didn't have crowds or streets to practise with. Just the Number One Line. So we walked up and down that – practising. We peeped modestly from underneath the felts, and every now and then raised a diffident hand in a small wave. My Fader watched sardonically from the cow paddock. He imitated our small waves. A faint hoot of laughter reached us in the chill wind.

'Don't look,' hissed Cherry in my ear, 'he is vulgar.'

I looked wistfully at Far. I would have given much to ask him to do his imitation, for Cherry, of the Duke of Gloucester travelling up the Foxton Line in his large black car on his recent triumphant tour of New Zealand. The populace had been warned to stay by their posts on the edge of the road and wave as the Duke toured slowly past. Even though the Duke had forgotten to tour slowly past, my Fader's keen eye had marked every detail – that slow wave, the Duke's well-built figure, the well-sprung car . . . Far did the Duke of Gloucester every night after dinner.

Coronation Day

We trailed inside to my bedroom and stood aimlessly in front of my dressing-table mirror. Cherry muttered, 'Princess Elizabeth and Princess Margaret Rose arrive at the Wembly Stadium to attend the Military Tattoo.'

We gazed fixedly at ourselves in the mirror and waved. 'Click,' said Cherry.

'You are the throne-followers?' asked an intensely interested voice. Cherry jumped, then hung her head. She found it difficult to actually look at my Bedstemoder. It was the pulled-back hair, she had kindly explained to me, the cheek-bones, and the rings flashing on those long bony fingers. *Viking* rings, Cherry had breathed. Her eyes had been round and anxious. She had gathered the information from here and there, that the Vikings had actually eaten children in the olden days. I had laughed – and that, of course, had made it worse. Deep under our mushroom hats we gazed at my Bedstemoder.

'Look,' she said, having difficulty with the 'oo' sound, as usual, 'I have found this for you.'

She thrust under our noses a very black photograph album. On one page a sturdy, oil-stained young man grinned at us from his seat in a very small boat. He had his cap on back to front.

'Danish throne-follower – Frederick!' said my Bedstemoder in a ringing voice. 'He is good fellow. Always telling stories and drinking snaps with the people. He is good boat man.'

Cherry took in the Danish Throne-Follower with one bleak peep.

'The English Royal Family don't drink snaps, Mrs Westergaard,' said my brave, loyal Cherry. Then she went as pink as a real English rose when my Bedstemoder started on her laugh.

The next week was the Coronation. For months Miss Martin had told us about coronations. On Coronation Day, Miss Martin said, we were to come to school only for a little while. We were to have Assembly and *receive a present from the King*! Then we were to celebrate with our families, each in our simple way, explained Miss Martin, in a manner that would please the King.

On 12 May 1937 Cherry met me at our gate. We had on our Royal outfits. I had had a little tussle of wills with my Moder, who asked me how could we go to our picnic dressed as if to go shopping in town? 'We are to dress for the Coronation,' I told her. I could not tell her that I had turned into the Princess Elizabeth, and that, at Assembly, heavenly voices would sound from the skies and Cherry and I would walk out to greet our people, sparing a kindly thought for the multitude of loyal subjects scattered over the world in our father's Dominions.

At school, Miss Martin whiled away the time before the Coronation Assembly by giving us, once again, the story about Princess Elizabeth in our Standard One *Journal*. Cherry was called upon to read. She stood up, invisible under her hat, and read again the words we knew by heart:

> Princess Elizabeth began her birthday by going for a ride on her pony with her father, the Duke of York, and Princess Margaret Rose. Later on in the day she had a tea-party, at which she blew out the candles on her iced cake. She then cut the first slice of the cake and handed it to her father. After tea, she went, as a birthday treat, to the moving pictures.

Handed it to her father. How dignified. Went to the moving pictures! Not the flicks with all that yelling and running about of the matinée audience.

'I wonder what the little Princesses are doing – this very moment,' said Cherry, as we stood in our serried ranks on the school tennis courts.

'All over the world,' shouted the Headmaster, warming up, 'boys – and girls – are turning their most fervent thoughts towards that great city, London, where at this very moment . . .' He paused and consulted his wrist-watch. He frowned. Then he got back into his stride, '. . . where soon our King will be enthroned.'

Enthroned. We gazed sternly at the flag hanging in the autumn sun from its noble pole. The Standard Six boy started his drum rattle; we sang, and the next moment we were shuffling out of the school gate, clutching our free Coronation pencils stamped with flags and crowns.

And there was our car – the Dodge – looking frightfully shabby, and full of our picnic lunch, and Far and Mor and Bedstemoder and

Bor the dog, looking fearfully ordinary. It was a strange day, to go bowling down the gravel road over the Plains to Foxton Beach for our Coronation Picnic, when we should be doing the Sums, the Spelling . . .

The Princesses Elizabeth and Margaret Rose, heads modestly bowed, stepped into the Royal Dodge.

'Don't trip,' cried my Bedstemoder in a vulgar voice. Then she thought better of it. 'You have pencils there, I see,' she said.

'King George the Sixth gave us these pencils,' said Cherry repressively. She held on to hers tightly in case the Viking-Dronning would snatch it, and eat it for her dinner. We both gazed out of the windows of the Dodge, regal underneath our mushroom hats. We longed to raise one gloved hand each to acknowledge the cheers of the Coronation crowds lining the road on either side, but dared not, in case my Bedstemoder once more broke the spell.

Then we saw the rabbit. It streaked up the road before us. And Fader turned before our very eyes into a Viking.

'Charge!' he shouted. He pressed his foot on the accelerator. We reached fully thirty miles per hour. Moder laughed.

'Bor!' yelled Fader. 'Rabbit!' And Bor did his leap; his great rabbit leap. Straight through the side-curtain window he crashed, bowled over and over in the dust, and plunged like a tiger through the long grass after that rabbit. Cherry screamed, Far braked, and we lurched to a stop.

Royal hat over one eye, Cherry said in a loud, indignant voice, '*Some*body has taken my King's pencil.'

We all tumbled out into the road. The Manawatu Plains lay all around us, bland, heavy, silent. There were no heavenly voices, no trumpet calls for the Coronation. Just that silence.

Centennial Exhibition

In 1940, through the kindly help of Tante Helga and the Centennial Exhibition, I became a member of my Nation – New Zealand. It was the school pad that started it. At school, we had gone on to pads. And, in 1940, the pads blossomed into pictures on their covers. New Zealand pictures. I gazed at my new pad. On the bottom was a sad bird looking at me sideways from a tree. The words underneath explained the bird's sad look. 'Huia,' they said, 'Now Extinct.' My heart ached for that bird, now vanished. But on the *top* of the cover, ah, my heart swelled. There were towers, banners, cumulus clouds, fountains. And across the fattest cumulus clouds was a banner of words: 'Centennial Exhibition – New Zealand – 1840–1940'

In Wellington, you could see those towers, those banners, those eagles and clouds. And one day, at Assembly, the Headmaster gave his simple, outraged announcement:

'The Education Board has decreed that all pupils who can procure the necessary money for their fares, will proceed, by train, to Wellington to view the Centennial Exhibition, escorted by their teachers and any parents who wish to come. Any child who misbehaves will be immediately expelled from the train at the most convenient stop and will then return home by the first conveyance going in that direction!'

Ha! There was dead silence. Who could procure the necessary monies for their fare, and not be expelled from the train as well? We eyed each other.

After school, I burst into the dining room at home, where

Centennial Exhibition

everyone was peacefully settling over their coffee and sugar cakes.

'We are to go,' I announced, 'on the train to Wellington to view the Centennial Exhibition. That is, if we are not first expelled from the train for riotously behaving!'

'Ah,' said Far, 'you can travel with the community of your fellow scholars. He carefully selected the biggest cake. 'But not,' he added, 'with that mob. Alone. They would scalp you before you reached Levin.'

'We are going later this year,' said my Moder.

'But think of the opportunity,' said Fader, 'travelling with her fellow students through the beautiful countryside, singing songs, and so on.'

'This is *not* Denmark,' said my Bedstemoder.

We ate our sugar cakes, deep in thought.

'We can be accompanied by an adult,' I added. Now I was using big words, as well as school pads.

'Helga!' cried my Fader, banging his fist on the table and making the cups dance. 'You love train journeys, Helga! You can sit with her and watch the goings-on from afar. And you can show her that special thing in the Exhibition as a surprise!'

Helga's cheeks turned pink. She began to plan the contents of our health-giving lunch.

On the day of the Exhibition trip we climbed into the train, far too early. Helga and I, burdened with our equipment, gazed at rows of empty seats, all beautifully stabbed with buttons.

'This is the Field's Train,' said Tante Helga. 'Your Grandonkel Nicolai-Frederik successfully tendered for the sleepers of this great railway track. We are to ride,' she said proudly, 'on Onkel Nicolai-Frederik's sleepers!'

I gazed apprehensively at the floor of the carriage.

'Wooden bars,' kindly explained Tante Helga, 'which bear the weight of the iron rails.'

We sat down in a corner, facing each other. Around us Tante Helga disposed our parcels.

'Provisions,' said Tante Helga, 'for the body *and* the mind.' She rummaged in a parcel. 'We may have a little something while we wait,' said Tante Helga.

The Bear from the North

I bit into one of her home-grown sandwiches. Wholemeal bread with the grains sticking out, and inside, something sticky, and chopped-up nuts.

'Honey . . .' said Tante in her religious voice, as she vigorously chewed, 'for energy.' I chewed seriously.

Down the station platform came the rhythmic tramp of marching feet. A whistle blew. Tante peeped gaily out of her window.

'There is a man with a funny hat on,' she said. 'He is blowing a whistle. There are big boys in conflict over something . . .'

I peeped out of my window. Big boys were hitting each other. The Headmaster, wearing what looked like his beach hat, was indeed blowing his whistle. There were thuds from the next carriage. The train rocked. Another whistle blew. You could hear a pin drop. Then, hushed as mice, through the carriage door came Mrs Taylor with Cherry, and Mrs Manners, with Georgie. Speaking in whispers, they put baskets on the seats, and sat neatly down.

'Good morning, Mrs Manners!' called Tante Helga, flushed with the gaiety of trains. 'Good morning, Mrs Taylor!'

'How d'ye do?' whispered Mrs Manners and Mrs Taylor. Then we all looked out of our windows, sombre with the prospect of long journeys and great discoveries.

A long, mournful whistle blew. The train began to move. Tears stung my nose. We were going to leave the Manawatu and all our loved ones far behind. Tante Helga tried to cheer me up.

'When all our family were setting forth on a trip to Levin to see the Rasmussens,' said Tante Helga in a loud ringing voice, 'we had tied up our good dog, Bor, at home. But Bor, says that dog to himself, now why shouldn't I go to see the Rasmussens too? So he slipped his chain, and set off, and came skip-hop, skip-hop, all the way down to the station. And Henning looked up and there was Bor, running along for dear life behind the train. And do you know –' Tante leaned forward and hit me smartly on one knee – 'that good faithful Bor ran all the way to Longburn behind the train! And the guard always said, No dogs allowed on trains. And Henning pounced on Bor at Longburn and the dog Bor hid himself behind my long skirts all the way to Levin and only peeped out once, and that guard, he never discovers that clever Bor was a passenger without a ticket!'

I opened my mouth. I gave my great bellow of a laugh. Mrs Taylor and Mrs Manners bowed their heads and looked quietly out of their windows.

Tante Helga rummaged briskly in another bag. Out came a book. She waved it in front of my dazzled eyes. 'Now it is time to *learn*!' cried Tante Helga. 'Journeys, they are for the education of the mind and the delight of the eyes!'

Tales of Maoriland for Little Folk said letters most skilfully twisted into shapes of what seemed to be supplejack on the book's cover. I opened it and read:

> Little Hemi opened his dusky eyes and gazed at the forest around him. He had slept late and already his friends, the birds of Tane's great trees, were hopping and chirping about his feet.

The train reached Levin. Little Hemi had met a new playmate, beautiful brown-eyed Tutanekai, who had been washing her face in a fern-fringed pool. I raised my eyes reluctantly from the page and gazed groggily out of the window. The Headmaster was striding down the platform, blowing his whistle at a group of boys struggling around a counter piled with thick mugs. A pie flew through the air. And there was Miss Martin, in a hat with veiling and a new suit, laughing with Miss Gore! Thunderstruck, I gazed at Miss Gore, laughing. I looked to see if Cherry had noticed. But Cherry was a changed girl. Travel had unnerved her group. Speaking in whispers, they were all hunched over a suitcase packed with food.

The train started again, and rocked Hemi and Tutanekai and I to sleep. I woke up. The train had stopped. An enormous notice board said OTAKI. And sitting in a group on the platform – I saw them – the hawk-faces, the Maoris. Tante Helga looked at me, and her face had changed, but she said nothing.

The train gathered itself together. We raced on past high hills and bush. The clouds arched over the sky, the train raced the clouds. And then the train screamed and burst out of a tunnel and there was the sea. And Wellington.

I clung to Tante Helga as we climbed up on to a tram. It moaned and swayed through a canyon edged with high buildings. On a crossing, I saw an amazing sight. There was our school, straggling in a long line, and out in the street, our own Headmaster, hat on the back of his head, whistle in his hand, imperiously trying to stop the traffic. The tram groaned on and left them far behind.

'Soon, soon,' shouted Tante Helga in my ear, 'I *show* you things.' And there it was, the Exhibition, laid out before us. We walked past fountains, arrowing to the sun. We walked up endless avenues, and there were the towers, the flags snapping in the wind. I craned my head to see the eagles and the cumulus clouds and I knew they were there. Then we were in a huge hall. We walked past giant logs of wood and pictures of Kauri trees. Helga seemed to be searching for something she knew was there. And then she stopped.

'Look, child!' she said, and her eyes shone. In a glass case, hanging by itself, was a long length of linen. Sequins, beads and shells flashed on it. And I knew it. I knew it. It was my Bedstemoder's embroidery of the ship – our ship – that we came on from Denmark. The long Viking shape, the scarlet dragon's breath, streaming in the wind. Tante Helga snatched my hand.

'Kom!' she said. 'You remember the Maoris we saw at Otaki?' She pointed. 'There is Kupe,' she said, 'the sea-traveller, the one who discovered New Zealand.'

I slowly raised my eyes. And there he was – high above our heads – the bronze Sea-God pointing over the sky to the land coming out of the mist – New Zealand. By his side stood a woman, as tall as our Danish women.

'These are our first people in this land,' said Tante Helga, her voice harsh and proud, 'they came in ocean canoes, built like our long-ships. Dragon-prowed. The Maori and the Dane, they knew how to travel the great seas.'

Behind me, my Bedstemoder's ship shone softly, dangerously, in the dim light. I clutched my health lunch in sweating hands. In that great hall people's voices made a murmuring sound. I looked up. Paua shell eyes slanted down at me, the Sea-God's face brooded over his people.

In my ears the train shrieked again and flung itself out of the tunnel straight at the triumphant sea.

The Woman from Norway

When I was eight my cousin Anna-Christina was flower-girl to Hanne Jacobsen. And that was when I first saw the Norwegian woman.

On the day of the wedding we arrived at the church door a little late. There was Anna-Christina, hair waved, face clean, frowning responsibly at her bouquet of autumn leaves. And in her hair autumn leaves also, an autumn-leaf wreath. *Artificial autumn leaves.* My mouth started to droop like a barn door hanging on one hinge. Before it could droop any further into its roaring shape, my Fader and Moder hustled me past. The grown-up bridesmaids were nice Danish girls. They bobbed their heads in greeting and gave us ceremonial bridesmaids' smiles. Later they all paced solemnly behind Hanne Jacobsen as she inched towards the altar and the gravity of marriage to Arne Thorvaldsen, but Anna-Christina never stopped posing with her artificial autumn-leaf wreath. And when she passed us on the way out she looked more married than Mr and Mrs Arne Thorvaldsen.

Then we went to the wedding feast. We sat at our half circle of tables as if we were really in a horned building in ancient Denmark waiting for the skjald's song, instead of in the lounge of Collinson and Cunningham, Broadway, Palmerston North. The skjald was a woman. She sat behind a tall stringed instrument. Her hair was in a low plait around her head. She leaned forward and touched a string. It gave out a single cold sound. And when I heard that sound I looked up. My Fader's face was shining. He leaned down to me.

'She plays the *harp*,' he hissed, 'as in olden days in Denmark.' The woman ran her hand up the strings, and drops of cold sound hung in the air. Then she sang and her voice was as cold, as full of our far-off lands as the harp sound. Everyone looked down at their hands, overcome with music. But one face gazed out over the singer's head. Two eyes as grey as rain surveyed a land they had never forgotten. And never would. I forgot Anna-Christina and her artificial autumn leaves. I gazed at that new face; and it looked at me. Incurious. Indifferent. The eyes took me in for a moment, and then glanced away, not shining like rain, but holding ice, the memory of winter.

At the end of the wedding feast, when the bride was restored to her everyday self again, tossing her veil back from her face, talking and laughing to people about this and that, Mor and Far and Tante Helga and I all moved as one person to that harp and its player. We stood around and talked about songs and how hard it would be to carry a harp and when had she come out from Denmark. And I stood and looked at the harp. Its strings stretched over my head, wrapped in their silver silence. I thought, it will have its own name, and its own history, as the great swords that our warriors carried into battle had their own names, their own renown.

Then, looking through the harp strings at me was that face, the one with the eyes that had been turned into ice. And that woman spoke to me, briefly, in a low, hoarse voice, with a faint, warning, dark 'r' sound.

'Do you sing?' she asked.

'I am beginning to,' I answered.

'I sing,' she said. 'My voice is very deep. Ja, in Norway I sang songs to many people.'

Nor-r-way. In her voice lived another person. Someone from a long time ago, a long-lost country, spoke in that voice – that woman – that ghost.

When we got home that night I said to Tante Helga, 'The woman from Norway spoke to me. By that harp. We talked about singing.'

Helga looked at Mor and Far. Nobody said a word, but that night Helga read me a story. One whole story – and a scrap of one.

'You want to know about Norwegians?' she asked. I nodded my head.

The Woman from Norway

'Ah,' said Helga, 'H. C. Andersen talks about Norwegians in this story called "Elfinmount". He tells us all about them.'

In that story elves spring-cleaned their home and practised their stamping dance. The Elf-King was expecting important guests, the old Troll-King of Norway and his sons, Mermaids, the Hell-Horse and the Night-Raven. Two of the Elf-King's daughters were going to be married to sons of the Troll-King. They were awful, those sons. They tickled their dinner partners, two young elf-maidens, with pine cones they had brought in their pockets. Then they took off their shirts and lay down on the table to sleep – for, as they said, they didn't stand on ceremony. but the old Troll-King spoke of Norway, the rivers and streams that leapt down the cliffs and sounded like both a thunderclap and an organ playing. Young people skated, carrying burning torches, with the fish in the ice beneath their feet fleeing in terror before them.

'Who is that Norwegian woman?' I suddenly asked.

'She is companion to your Grandtante Ingeborg. She came out of Norway some years ago.'

And that is all she would say. But in my dreams I saw the woman from Norway in the other story she told me that night, the short one. I saw a very different Norwegian from that old Troll-King.

The next year the Second World War began. Denmark was invaded, there was fighting in the mountains and fjords of Norway.

'Ah!' said my Bedstemoder. 'They still know how to fight there – those Vikings!'

We were sitting on the sand-hills at Foxton having a picnic. It was a strange, restless picnic. The weather was wrong and the sun was cooling silver. Fader and Onkel Sven and Onkel Henning could not keep still. They paced about, gazing out to sea, talking of the war in Norway. I trailed after Sven. We walked far beyond the others, then we sat down on a nice bit of sand.

'Tell us a story, Onkel Sven, tell us a story!' I nagged.

He was so good at telling stories, that one, you could see all the people in his words. But today, his eyes went restlessly down the beach to where the others were sitting. Then I saw her – the woman from Norway. She was sitting beside my Grandtante Ingeborg. They had both been knitting, but the Norwegian woman

The Bear from the North

had let her hands drop. She was gazing out to sea.

Onkel Sven looked very hard at her, then he said in a hurrying voice to keep me quiet, 'Ja. Well, once upon a time we had a Norwegian girl to look after us. She was straight out of a little village and Moder paid her passage and she worked for us. And she brought us all out into the sand-hills here to give the kitten his walk.'

'The kitten?'

'We had a kitten in a box. We brought him from Palmerston North when we came here for the summer. I let him out for a little walk. And we lost him.'

'Lost him?'

'Ja!' said Sven, savagely digging in the sand with a stick. 'We looked for days, but that kitten . . .'

'Sven . . .?'

'Ja,' said Sven. 'Four dopes, calling out to that kitten day and night. In Danish. But that Norwegian girl, she was so homesick, she came out at night and called the kitten, in Norwegian! Night after night. Then she would weep. She was as lost as the kitten. She went back to Norway later.'

'Who is she?' I asked.

Sven knew who I meant. He looked down at the distant figure sitting as still as a stone, looking out to sea.

'Don't you tell anyone I told you this,' muttered Sven, 'but Helga told me she gets an income from Norway. Very regular money. Her voice is trained and she went to a good school in Oslo. But when she was eighteen she was sent to us from Norway. And she was asked not to go back.'

'Not to go back?'

'Helga says,' said Sven, digging away with his stick, 'that her Moder was a servant girl in the palace at Oslo, and her Fader – never mind – never mind.'

I looked at the sea. Then I remembered the other story Helga had read to me on the night of the wedding. The scrap of the story by H. C. Andersen:

We have seen swans too, fly with powerful wings high up in the sky. One touched, with his wings, the golden harp, and the music

112

resounded through the north. The stark mountains of Norway rose high in the light from the ancient sun. The gods of the north and the heroes and heroines from the Viking age again walked in the deep green forest. But one swan, striving to fly home, beat its wings against the marble cliffs so hard that it died . . .

Sven looked at me.
'Her Fader and Moder weren't married,' he said briefly. Then he got up and walked away. But I had seen his eyes.

The Battle Charge

The beginning of the Second World War ... Assemblies outside in a high wind.

'All over the world,' shouted our grey Headmaster, 'soldiers, sailors and airmen of the Dominions are arming to go to the aid of our great Motherland. Your fathers, uncles and brothers will march to the call. We will never rest until the foe is swept to defeat. Children of this school will – each in his humble way – assist our gallant soldiers and sailors and airmen in bringing the foe to his knees ...'

I smiled at Cherry Taylor. Cherry Taylor smiled back. Marbles, said our eyes, at playtime ...

'Westergaard,' shouted the Headmaster, 'we will have no levity here! The *British* do not accept defeat as the European nations do. We are made of sterner stuff. Oh, yes! School – three cheers for Great Britain!'

Oh, how we cheered! Soldiers of the Dominions we were. Then we marched back to Miss Martin's room.

'Friis!' bellowed the Headmaster at Anna's elder brother Kjeld. 'Shoulders *back*, sir! Wipe off that smile!'

Then I discovered the true nature of the war. The school was fighting two foes. The Germans. And us! It started one playtime.

'Whitey!' hissed Avis Cameron. 'White-hair! Wolf-eyes! Hun!' I looked behind to see that wolf. Then I found Avis Cameron had her hands around my throat. It was a fun-fight! I made the grave error of laughing. Then Avis Cameron started strangling me.

'Lay off!' said a cold voice. And Anna Friis was strangling Avis

The Battle Charge

Cameron. Then the bell went, and they stopped. I panted after Anna.

'What are Hun, Anna?' I called.

'Sh-sh,' said Anna, looking nervously about. Then she put her mouth to my ear. 'The Germans came up through Holstein,' she whispered, 'but the Danish soldiers met them at the Jutland frontier. They fought. All were killed.'

Then she looked at me. I stared stupidly back. 'We fought!' said Anna impatiently.

'Your family lived in Holstein once, didn't they, Anna?' I gabbled.

'Sh-sh,' said Anna, 'we are South Jutland people. Only one Bedstemoder came from Holstein. Oh, that Slesvig-Holstein War was a muddle!' Our families had come to New Zealand after the war to get away from the Germans. They had occupied South Jutland. Now it was part of Denmark again.

'Anna has beautiful teeth,' my Fader said once. 'There is German blood there.' My Fader taught me the great truths about the European nations. The Dutch saved their nation from the sea that tried to drown them. The Russians in their icy nation knew how to defeat the cruel winters. And the Germans had made for me a nest of wooden bowls for my doll's house. They fitted exactly on the tips of my fingers. Those bowls gave my fingers the most wonderful feeling.

'They understand wood,' said my Far. 'All men have something precious to give the world.' And his face shone with pride to be part of the world, to be brother to all men.

'Peggy-squares for our soldiers and sailors and airmen,' said Miss Martin. 'Scraps of wool of bright colours to cheer them up in the battle fields. They need to have the prettiest colours!' Then she looked sad. Her young man would be going forth to the cruel wars.

We found the prettiest wool to comfort Miss Martin and cheer up our fighting forces.

At home the Grandonkels raised their glasses of snaps before dinner.

'To our brave lille Denmark!' they rumbled. 'To Konge

Christian of the Danes!' Their eyes gleamed ice-blue with tears as they saw the King on his horse riding with all the Danes on their bicycles through the snowy Copenhagen streets lined with German soldiers.

Then Anna Friis and I fell in love with Conrad Veidt. He was on the films at the Regal Picture Theatre in his poor submarine. It looked a bit like an old fish tin; it needed mending. But Conral Veidt was so harried by the perils of the sea that he had not time to mend it! He kept pacing about in his streaming oilskins, peering through binoculars over the cold North Sea. We didn't tell each other that it was his eyes that we loved. They were the eyes of our Northern people, with the look of the sea in them. In the end Conrad Veidt slowly sank with his submarine. The sea came up to his chest, the rain poured down, and Conrad Veidt slowly and sadly saluted Europe farewell. We wept so much that we couldn't see anything outside the Regal Picture Theatre in the bright unfeeling afternoon sun. We rode our bikes home, wiping the tears away and laughing in hollow voices. But I was thinking of Conrad Veidt and the tiny figures of those Danish soldiers running across the Jutland fields to try to stop the German army crossing the frontier. And so was Anna.

Then came the day of the Air Raid Practice.

'On the signal of the school bell,' shouted the Headmaster, 'you will proceed at a smart run, *and* in an orderly fashion, through the gate into the mustering paddock. You will select a suitable hollow that will protect you from a blast. You will lie down and place your rubber between your teeth and the cotton-wool tufts in both ears, left and right. Then you will lie *perfectly still*. There will be no talking. Anybody who talks will get a taste of my strap. When you hear the whistle you will rise to your feet, remove the rubber from between your teeth and the cotton wool from your ears. You will then march back to your classrooms with *no talking*.'

Miss Martin kindly translated his directions. 'The mustering paddock, dears,' she said, 'is the pony paddock. Do not on any account lie too near Phyllis Blake's Shetland pony. He kicks.'

The Battle Charge

The school bell rang like a call to battle. We trotted happily down to the pony paddock, talking of this and of that. We clenched our rubbers between our teeth and became miraculously deaf with the white cotton wool. Then we lay neatly down in the hollow of our choice, well away from Phyllis Blake's kicking Shetland pony. And do you know what we found close to our refuge? Sour grass! We ate and ate. Then, up by the big boys' hollows, we heard someone laugh.

'Friis!' bellowed the Headmaster. 'We will have no Continental levity here, sir! March to my room now.'

The long figure of Kjeld Friis unfolded from the grass. He didn't march though – he walked like an absent-minded cat.

At the end of school that day, Cherry and Anna and Kjeld and I gathered at our bikes for the ride home. There was no one about, which was strange.

'They've gone to the settlement to see if there are soldiers there,' said Anna.

The gale was blowing. It was a head wind all the way home. Kjeld rode behind, fooling around as usual. Then Cherry saw them.

'There are lots of children there,' said Cherry. We slowed down. A long line of children was stretched across the road. Avis Cameron was in the front.

'Hun!' shouted Avis.

'What?' yelled Cherry.

'Hun!' shouted Avis, somewhat louder.

'What are Hun, Astrid?' asked Cherry. But Kjeld Friis had suddenly caught up to us.

'Ride!' he yelled. 'Ride like hell!'

And we charged. Oh, how we charged! I got my steel-lined Raleigh bike up to battle speed in *ten yards*.

'What are Hun, Astrid?' called Cherry again.

'Ride, Cherry!' yelled Kjeld, and his voice cracked. We stood on our pedals and charged like the wind. Straight through that line we rode.

'Cut off the Huns at the cross road!' Avis Cameron shouted. She mounted her bicycle. I laughed and rode right into the nor'wester with the others. And there was my Fader out on the road, waiting for us. He had one of the wooden rattles off the Christmas tree in his hand. He rattled it at Kjeld.

'The winner!' he yelled. 'New Zealand's golden hope for the National Cycling Champs!'

'Mr Westergaard,' shouted Kjeld, circling round Far in his joy, 'The school called us Huns and tried to stop us from coming home, but we charged them!'

'Up us Huns!' shouted Cherry.

Then my Fader ran frantically out into the road.

'Where are they?' he shouted. He shook the rattle fiercely over his head. It made a thin sound in the booming wind. Then a terrible thing happened. He let the rattle droop in his hand – and he wept.

The Young Kings

When the Second World War came we were training to be actresses. Not yet on the stage, but in good acting places which we found at home. We didn't act on the surface of ourselves; we changed entirely into somebody else. We changed, mostly, into cowboys. The back lawn got very dry in the summer and there was a delicious suggestion of crackling sage-brush underfoot.

Anna Friis galloped up on a phantom horse, climbed down and tethered it. We tiptoed towards each other in our phantom cowboy boots, toes turned inward, and Anna drawled, 'Wa-al, this sure is a one-horse burg for someone the likes of me to sojourn in, stranger . . .'

Then I growled, 'Sa-ay, pardner, where you come from this shining morn?' (Our cowboy speech was mixed with the everyday speech of the gods and heroes of Asgaard.)

We looked accusingly at Cherry Taylor, cowering by the edge of lawn.

'What do I *say*, Astrid – what do I *say*?' she beseeched.

We had become quite practised in cementing over gaps in the ongoing drama. I called out, very rapidly, 'O-ho, pardner, you say, this burg is too small for the likes of you, is it? and I say, I am the Mayor of this town and whence come you from?'

'What?' Cherry piped.

'Say,' Anna chanted, coldly spacing out the words, 'Oho – pardner – this – burg – is – too – small – for – the – likes – of – you – is – it . . .'

The Bear from the North

Then we gave up, and cantered slowly round and round the lawn, wailing,

> O-old Faithful, we ri-ide the ra-ange together,
> O-old Faithful, in an-y kind of wea-ther!

And Cherry joined in happily on a phantom Shetland pony, and not on one of those fearful bolting cowboy nags, as she described them, that Anna and I rode.

'I like action!' said Anna Friis. 'Galloping horses, and so on.'

I knew what she meant. For we were both secretly in love with the King of the Danes who was pictured with his horse on the title page of old Saxo's *Gesta Danorum*. The King had died before 1220, when Saxo Grammaticus died too, but that didn't matter. We gazed at that Danish King. He had long blond hair, a face that shone with light, and he held the sceptre in one hand, an upraised sword in the other, and over his armour was a long embroidered cloak. But, above all, he stood with his feet apart and he was wearing the silver Danish crown *at a rake helly angle*. Now a silver crown set at a rake helly angle on long blond hair is an irresistible sight.

So we pestered Far to read us old Saxo's stories to glean some precious information about that Danish King, but Far was useless!

He would frown at old Saxo's heavy Danish print and mutter, 'Now let me see – let me see. It says here – now let me see – the King galloped up to this man's house and they said . . . Well, anyway, they were being challenged by another man, so in the early morning the King and his friends went off on their horses, and they met the other man and his sons – and there was a fight. Hang on, hang on – yes – it says here that the King rode back with the first man. Then they had breakfast.'

'*Had breakfast?*'

'Well,' said Fader, 'they liked their food in those days, too. Typical Danes, always thinking of their stomachs.'

'Fader!'

Helga came to our rescue.

'Asgaa-aard!' hissed Helga, waving Saxo and the easier book of Norse legends at us. She read,

The Young Kings

In the beginning of time, there was nothing. Neither sand, nor sea ... In the morning of the northern world, before history was, there dwelt in Scandinavia a mighty race of men and women. From the stars they learned the magic of runes. With these they ruled the winds, stilled the sea and quenched fire ...

Ah! That was more like us! Then she read to us of a god called Baldur.

He was so beautiful and bright that he glowed with white fire. He was the most beloved of the gods, and he loved all things. His gold arm ring was called Draupnir.

We savoured those words 'white fire'. We peeped at the young King, Rex Danorum. His face glowed with white fire too. So we fell in love with both Baldur, the Shining One, and Rex Danorum.

We dressed up like the Danish King, with a dash of Baldur. We made Baldur's arm ring, Draupnir, out of a broad blade of grass, and knotted quilts around our necks. We galloped swift as the wind up and down the paddock on phantom horses, waving the wooden swords that Fader had made for us. Cherry made a broom into a horse and galloped up and down on that. She was a lady, she said, riding a white horse. We went on shouting bits of Danish and carrying out our battle charges. When we got tired of battles, we rode our bikes up and down the road, cloaks flapping, and sang, 'I'm Mad About Music!' exactly as Deanna Durbin had sung it, on a bicycle, through orchards in bloom, in the film *Mad About Music*. Sometimes we rang our bicycle bells in rhythmic accompaniment. Deanna Durbin always had a full symphony orchestra accompanying *her*, wherever she might be, in field or orchard or open road. We missed that sorely. At the end we shouted, 'Charge! Rex Danorum! Baldur the Shining!' and belted up the road, cloaks streaming behind.

One day in 1942 Anna and I were sitting on the bridge over the creek which ran through our garden. We wore our quilt cloaks and our Draupnirs, as usual, but our wooden swords we laid beside us. We took in the summer silence of the land, the dried-up creek.

Then I blinked. A large clump of cocksfoot *was moving towards us*.

'Anna,' I said hoarsely. Then my mouth dropped open. Three clumps of cocksfoot were moving up the creek towards us. We gripped our swords. The cocksfoot clumps came on steadily and, just in front of us, tilted back. And underneath each bunch of grass was a soldier's face. Very grim. They looked at us coldly. Anna rose to the occasion.

'Good morning,' she said very nicely to the first cocksfoot clump.

It looked briefly at her, then dipped forward and crawled busily underneath our bridge. Quick as a flash I hung my head over the other side to meet it crawling out.

'Good morning,' I said, upside-down.

'Goddam it,' said the cocksfoot clump and vanished up the creek, followed bumpily by the other cocksfoot clumps, who all swore one way or another as they met the netting barrier my Fader had cleverly put up to strain bits of branches and grass out of the floods. Then there were no more cocksfoot-crowned soldiers.

'Come on,' said Anna, grabbing my hand. She raced me to where we had parked our bikes by the front fence.

'Anna!' I gasped as we wrestled with our cloaks to get our feet on the pedals. 'Anna – what were those men doing?'

'Warriors,' said Anna, 'practising war.'

Like the Danish King and his friends! Like the gods and heroes of Asgaard!

Anna was charged with the ferocity of battles. She stood on her pedals, rang her bell and belted out 'I'm Mad About Music!' It was hard to catch up with her, but I did. Up and down we rode, circling, bell-ringing, singing, and now and again waving our swords and yelling 'Rex Danorum! Baldur the Shining!' Then, in the middle of a very good charge, cloak flapping, I had a strange feeling in the back of my head. I ground to a halt, clumsily stood in the stony road and squinted into the blinding summer light. And there, slumped deep in the dry grass at the side of the road for as far as I could see, were *hundreds* of men dressed in cocksfoot crowns and green uniforms. And they were all staring at us.

'Anna!' I shouted.

'Rex Danorum!' yelled Anna, circling very boldly.

The Young Kings

And out of that tired army, a tall, thin young man with a shining face and blond hair, his cocksfoot crown at a rakish angle, suddenly leapt to his feet and called, 'Old Saxo! Well, I'll be damned!'

That stopped us.

Where had that army come from? America. To save us from the Japanese. What was the young soldier's name? Ib Jensen. Slim for short. Where had he come from? From the Corn Belt of America – from a Danish community like ours.

Oh, how we loved him! He came weekend after weekend, and ate my Moder's aeblekager, my Moder's rødgrød. He told us about the Danes sailing to America. And about the first Scandinavian sea-traveller there – somebody called Eric the Red. We showed him Rex Danorum in old Saxo's book. His family had that book, he said. We looked at the face of the dead young Danish King and Ib's face. We both fell in love with Ib.

He gave us chewing gum and chocolate. He sang us old Danish songs. One day he translated the story of Baldur into easier words for us. He made me read it –

One day Baldur's shining face was sad, and his father Odin and his mother Friga begged him to tell them why. 'I have had three strange dreams which make me afraid,' said Baldur. 'First I dreamed that a black cloud came over the sun and shut out all its brightness. Then I dreamed that Asgaard was dark and that all the gods wept. The third night I dreamed that a voice in Asgaard cried, 'Weep, weep, Baldur the Beautiful is dead.'

Our faces fell.

'Never mind' said Ib comfortingly. 'Baldur rose from the dead and came back. Look at this poem.'

Anna read –

> Unsown field,
> Will grow rich with corn.
> And ills will get better,
> Baldur will come.

Ib pointed up the road at Mr Bell's farm. 'Like that corn,' he said.

'Baldur grows into life with corn. We planted the whole country with it at home.'

We gazed complacently at Mr Bell's one small wheat paddock.

Then Ib told us movie-land secrets about Deanna Durbin, about Shirley Temple. How they were just fun-loving girls going to school every day – like us!

He was killed in the invasion of an island in the Pacific. We watched Mr Bell's wheat spring up year after year, but he never came back.

Astrid of the Limberlost

Our school was divided into many groups, like the nations of the world. Some fought great battles against each other and then made loud treacherous Peace Treaties. These groups were the Gangsters. They spent playtimes and lunchtimes crawling through thickets of hydrangeas and shrubs seizing victims. Cherry Taylor was seized once. Anna Friis crawled into the hydrangeas and grabbed Cherry by her other arm.

'Release your victim, you nincompoop,' said Anna Friis in her cold, still voice. And the Gangsters, confused by Anna's long words, let her go. The Gangsters were always confused by long words. Inside school they drooped and died when it came to the *Journal* readings. We read in turn, one sentence each. A bumpy road it was; first one Gangster – then another – stumbled on in their poor hoarse voices. The first Gangster announced 'Angela's Cold'.

'At first you could hardly tell it was a sneeze, it was such a tiny one.' He dropped into his seat as if he had been shot. Then another Gangster clambered to his feet.

'Angela tried hard to think it was not one; but when it came again, it did indeed seem like a sneeze.'

He too dropped as if he had been shot. Then the biggest Gangster stood up with hunched shoulders like Pretty Boy Floyd. He growled –

'Just then Mother came in and pulled up the blind. "Good morning, Angela," she said, "slip on your dressing gown and run along to the bathroom".'

The Headmaster watched from his table by the fire. The strap lay by his hand. I leaned back and admired the scene. It was straight from *Les Misérables* by Victor Hugo – the flickering light from the fire, the high windows, the grey winter afternoon and a distant sound from the road outside of somebody breaking stones . . .

After the Gangsters had stumbled into silence, a representative of the next group stood up. This was the Grown-Up Girls' Group. She balanced on her high heels, bit her lip and tossed back her Ginger Rogers' hair-do. She wore a great many bits of her Moder's jewellery and pink fingernails made by colouring them in with a red pencil. She read in a wonderful, highly offended lisp:

'An-ge-la began to say some-thing, but a . . .'

'Middle-sized,' grated the Headmaster.

'Middle-sized,' lisped the Grown-Up Girl, 'sneeze stopped her.'

She tinkled some bangles on her arm.

I regarded her through half-closed eyes. Anna Karenina. A head crammed with pretty trifles, and that railway track at the end. At breaks I hung around the Grown-up Girls, observing them. The Grown-Up Girls longed for their last day at school. And until that day came, they practised. They wore stockings and shoes with highish heels, so they could not run. They spent the breaks slowly writing, in fancy letters, 'By hook or by crook I am first in this book' in each other's autograph albums, and they did each other's hair, absorbed in combing and fluffing, with hairpins clenched savagely in their teeth.

The rest of us, who were not Gangsters or Grown-Up Girls, ranged around looking for something to read. We tried the school library, a small grim storeroom, where the barred windows had ivy growing over them. There were two rows of thick black books. When we picked them up they fell open with a sigh of years and dampness, letting fall small, dead, transparent spiders. My book had on its opening page –

'What's your name?'

'Diggory Trevanock.'

The whole class exploded. This incident, one of the little pleasantries occasionally permitted by a class master, and which, like a judge's jokes in court, are always welcomed as a momentary relief from the depressing monotony of the serious business in hand, happened in the Second Class of a small preparatory school, situated on the outskirts of the market town of Chatford, intended for the sons of gentlemen.

I shut the book.

But at home, Tante Helga had a little surprise: a whole box of books someone had given her.

'*Girls*' books,' said Tante Helga, 'of the Colonies, the Antipodes and so on.' Already she was deep in a book. She waved vaguely at the heap, while I peeped at the cover of her book. *The Family at Misrule* said letters cleverly constructed from branches of a tree. There was a picture of a gentleman in boots striding out of a house on fire. He had a beaming baby in his arms. Did that baby not know that its house was on fire? Underneath, more tree branches said: by Ethel Turner.

'Try that one,' said Tante Helga in a vague, drugged voice. She gestured at a khaki book with black irises on it. *The Girl of the Limberlost*, said flowing, scarlet letters.

'What is Limberlost?' I asked.

Tante's eyes raced along the lines of her book, her lips moved. She surfaced only enough to give a taste of the family at Misrule.

'Nell is letting down her muslin,' said Tante mysteriously. 'Too young. She is but fifteen. Meg is distressed. Nell walks up and down. Frou-frou go the muslin frills above her shoes. The Cook likes Nell's new long dress.'

'Who is Cook?'

'They are English aristocrats,' said Tante. 'A lady cooks their food. She says things like "La Miss Nell." Now please read your *Limberlost* . . .' Her voice trailed away. She would read without breathing, without food, without sleep, until the book was finished. Then she would be the heroine for two days. Then she would be Tante Helga again.

I started my *Limberlost* saga. I read of a white-faced girl, forced to go to school by her cruel Moder, wearing thick boots, a shabby black hat, and a skimpy calico waist, whatever that was, and carrying a tin bucket with her lunch in it, to a new high school in some place called the city. My eyes raced along like Tante Helga's. The girl, Elnora, white-faced, but crowned with shining dark red hair, walked blinded by tears, climbed a snake fence and went along a trail worn by feet of men who guarded the precious timber of the swamp – *with guns*.

'Tante,' I quavered.

'Mmm,' murmured Tante.

'Tante . . .'

Helga raised blind eyes. She murmured, 'Meg has been left to look after the whole family. She teaches the little ones and wrestles with the Cook.'

'Fighting!' My heart stopped.

'Nej, nej,' said Helga impatiently. 'Disputes. About the food that is to be cooked.'

'What did they eat Helga? What did they eat?' Helga looked brighter.

'Lots of meat – boiled meat and roasted meat. The heat in Sydney it is not to be borne. The blow-flies get at the meat. The Cook is angry. Meg is distracted. Then they had . . .' With animation, Helga flipped through the pages. 'Ah!' she said. 'Beef-steak pie, sweet potatoes and a Cabinet Pudding. No greens!' said Tante Helga, scandalised.

'In my book,' I said excitedly, riffling pages, 'there is a dainty lunch baked by her kind aunt to make her respectable before her new classmates who wear dainty dresses and hair ribbons and scorn the Girl of the Limberlost. In her new leather lunchbox. Listen!' I read, getting hungrier and hungrier –

'Half the bread compartment was filled with dainty sandwiches of bread and butter sprinkled with the yolk of egg, and the rest with three large slices of the most fragrant spice cake imaginable. The meat dish contained shaved cold ham of which she knew the quality. The salad was tomatoes and celery and the cup held preserved pear, clear as amber. There were two tissue-wrapped cucumber pickles.

'And then she says – Tante Helga? Tante Helga? Listen! This bit says,

'She glanced around her and then to her old refuge, the sky. "She does love me!" cried the happy girl. "Sure as you're born my little Mother loves me!" '

I went to get a drink of water to offset the thought of the cucumber pickle, which would undoubtedly burn the mouth. I read on, leaning against the sink, swigging great gulps of artesian water. Elnora did chores after supper. It was ten o'clock when the chickens, pigs, and cattle were fed, the turnips were hoed and a heap of bean vines was stacked by the back door . . . At four o'clock next morning Elnora was shelling beans. At six she fed the chickens and pigs, swept the cabin, built a fire, and put on the kettle for breakfast . . .

I felt so tired that I went into my room and lay down on my bed to give me strength for the next bit. Worse was to come. To get dress-goods, shoes, hat and books for school Elnora had to comb the swamp, and find moths, butterflies and arrow heads. These she sold to somebody called the Bird Woman who lived in the city, but the Indian arrow heads she sold to the manager of the Bank of America. The money gained thereby, Elnora stashed into a hollow log, and brooded a little upon the swamp which was lying in God's glory about her. That night, saying her prayers, she noticed lights flashing by her hollow log, far off in the muck and ooze of the swamp.

I looked at those words, 'muck and ooze', and went to find my Fader.

'Far,' I quavered, 'where is the Great Swamp?' Fader straightened and swept an arm from horizon to horizon.

'Aw,' he said, 'all around us really. What a time they had!'

'Time?'

'Draining it, and so on,' said Fader cheerfully. 'But those Danes, my word, how they *worked* . . .'

'Far.'

'Ja?'

'Will we have enough money for me to go High school in the city?'

'Mmm,' said Fader, 'well – you'll have to work your fingers to the bone, be a model child and laugh at all my jokes . . .'

It was enough. I trailed to my bedroom and read a little more.

Elnora was weeping to her uncle about her cruel Moder. Her uncle explained –

'You see,' said Uncle Wesley, 'I was the first man there, honey. She just made an idol of him, your father, I mean. There was that oozy green hole, with thick scum and two or three bubbles slowly rising that were the breath of his body. There she was in spasms of agony, and beside her the great heavy log she'd tried to throw him. That's why she just loses control of her soul in the night, and visits that pool, and sobs and calls and begs the swamp to give him back to her . . .'

I shut that book so quickly, and lay and looked at the ceiling. Tante Helga drifted in with *The Family at Misrule* slackly between finger and thumb. Tante Helga was sated with goings-on and happy endings.

'What happened?' I asked glumly.

Tante Helga said in a tired-out voice, 'Ja, well, Nell went to dinner unlawfully at the home of a new-rich neighbour when Meg said Do not go. They are vulgar. Their cook had diphtheria. The only ornament poor Nell wore was a knot of wild flowers tucked in her bosom. She carried the diphtheria home. Little Esther caught it, Meg caught it. Poor Nell wept in the moonlight and prayed to God that the crisis would come.'

'The crisis was still to *come*?'

'The crisis,' explained Tante Helga with dignity, 'is when the body throws off the poisons of the fever and the skin gleams with sweat. Then they hug each other and praise God. Bunty the boy did not break the school window or steal the five sovereigns and was found months later, washing dishes at a low eating house in Sydney. The family is happy at last and thanks God yet again.'

'Ah,' I said, and rolled on to my stomach. Tante Helga arose. 'Dinner now!' she said, and went. I noticed she had a small bunch of wild flowers tucked into her bosom.

I gazed bleakly at the distant bush. Tomorrow I would have to start trying to find the Great Swamp of the Manawatu. Then I would start the arduous task of collecting moths, butterflies and Indian arrow heads, dodging the pool covered with green slime, around which my Moder paced at night calling my Fader's name. I would spy on the flickering lights of the Carson Gang signalling to each other where the best Redwoods were for smuggling out, and finally trudge along the twenty miles to the High School in Palmerston North, carrying my bucket of lunch and a load of Indian arrow heads carefully bunched in my skirt to sell to the Manager of the Bank of New Zealand, to pay for the books, dry goods, and my tuition. It would be a terrible life, but with grit and spunk I would pull through. As I knocked on the door of the Bank of New Zealand I could see a faint curve of sadness on my young lips, half concealing a smile – one for sweet buried childhood, and one for the broadening days.

The Headmaster

One day in the War Miss Martin went away. It happened suddenly. One weekend she just up and got married to that young man with the big rucksack and the floppy straw hat. He was called up and she was going to follow him, everyone said, to be near his camp.

We gave her a honey-pot. It was the most beautiful honey-pot we had ever seen – *golden* – with brown busy-bees perched all over it, and an extra large busy-bee perched on the lid. You grasped him and pulled, and he revealed the honey within. Miss Ogilvie of the Fancy Goods and Stationery Shop said it was quite the most tasteful piece of stock she had had in for many a long day. Marvelling at this peep into the world of commerce, we carried it away, quarrelling about whose turn it was to carry it next.

When it was time to say goodbye and hand over the honey-pot, there was Miss Martin, with red eyes and her tulip dress, and, beside her, her young man. It was a windy glittery day, and the dust flying over the Plains and whirling into the corners of the playground buffeted us and reddened our eyes and left us confused and silent. Miss Martin's young man was dressed in a khaki suit that was made for somebody much bigger. He stood stiffly with his eyes fixed on the back wall as if a big voice had shouted Attention! and he was too muddled and tired to stand at ease. He had always drifted along, that one, looking at the world with bright eyes.

Miss Martin peeped at the honey-pot. Then she slowly lifted the biggest busy-bee and looked inside for a long time. She said not a word, but hung on to it, with the tissue paper wrapping trailing

The Headmaster

down all untidy, and looked at us as we sang 'Butterfly, High in the Sky'. We had no song about bees. The wind beat at the windows and drowned her words when she spoke. All I can remember are our eyes red with grit and tears, and confusion. The wind was too much for us that day.

Then our chairs were stacked on top of our tables, bumpy with dried glue, and the door was locked behind us. Our old room was left to the silence of long empty afternoons and the sigh of summer pines and winter rain.

We were marched off with our bulging bags like foot soldiers off to the cruel wars. We went over the tennis courts and down the steps, and then up some steps into our grey Headmaster's senior room, and left Miss Martin and our world behind for ever.

The senior classes and the Headmaster drove home the reality of Facts to Miss Martin's class. There we sat in alphabetical order, encased in iron desks too big for us. T for Taylor sat in a corner, only the hair ribbons showing. F for Friis sat in front, white plaits quite still. And W for Westergaard sat at the back, turned back into that bear from the North whose families ate raw fish in the winter.

'What were the names of the principal canoes?' shouted the Headmaster. Oh, how the seniors cracked their fingers. Oh, how they groaned with the weight of their knowledge.

'Awatea!'
'Rangitane!'
'Ngapuhi!'
'Tainui!'

'What was the cause of Rewi's quarrel with the Governor?' More groans, more whip-cracking fingers.

I very cautiously slid my eyes upwards to the pictures on the wall beside me. A lady with a frilly bonnet and a look of suffering had one finger raised to a pack of crouching wild-women. I looked at the writing underneath. 'Elizabeth Fry Ministers to Prisoners in Newgate,' it said. I looked at an old, framed photograph, brown with age. A row of anxious boys sat among tree stumps, cross-legged and with arms tightly folded. A bare wooden shed rose behind them. With a kind of slow shock I recognised that shed. It was our old classroom. My eyes flew to the teacher standing with one hand on his hip, the other fiercely clutching a book. That teacher was only a little older than the boys. His face was strained and white with fear of the boys and the tree stumps and the teaching. And my face felt like his.

'Have you got your Rewi money?' asked Cherry anxiously one morning. I was so clumsy after Miss Martin vanished. I forgot everything and simpered at the Headmaster, which made him angrier than ever. Cherry checked me over every morning before school, to make sure I had my pencil and had learned my spelling words.

The Headmaster called me Westigid; I was too stupid to be called Astrid any more. I knew that when I was not stupid any more I would be called Astrid again. I kept thinking of Milly-Molly-Mandy's nice white cottage and planning how I would live in it, safe for ever away from school. I would just sit in the cottage and not have to see people at all, and get on their nerves.

'We are going to the *pictures*, Astrid,' said Cherry. 'You remember, *Rewi's Last Stand*.' Usually I loved the Regal Picture Theatre. It stood tall and stark in the middle of the settlement with its corrugated iron back and noble wooden front. You could see the Regal Picture Theatre for miles in the clear light burning over the farmlands and the flax-lands and the sand-hill country out by the coast. And the glitter and smell of those lands waited for us each Saturday afternoon outside the double doors of the picture theatre and its darkness and banging seats, where Miss Audrey Littlewood showed us to our places in a storm of bangles and perfume and waved hair and darting torch beam. And afterwards we rode home on our bikes over the gravelled roads. The light flashed its sword on the flax blades in the ditches, on the grass-waves in the paddocks, and we were Shirley Temple in *The Littlest Rebel* and Jane Withers in *Mrs Wiggs of the Cabbage Patch* and Tex Morton riding his horse, all the way home.

That day the school marched down to the Regal Picture Theatre to see *Rewi's Last Stand*. By the ditch in the school road an old man burned grass in a sulky fire. The smoke rose slowly to heaven and the drummer boy beat his slow tuck like a heavy heartbeat. People in the houses crouched like dwarfs came out to their gates to see us

The Headmaster

go by. But nobody waved.

'Keep inside your ranks,' shouted the Headmaster on the theatre steps. I clutched Cherry's hand. Miss Audrey Littlewood, responsible and frowning, stood at the door, preparing for our army to invade her theatre. There was a crashing roar of seats banging down and we sat perched in the darkness in complete silence. Cherry's hair ribbons stuck out quite motionless. From the back came the Headmaster's voice.

'Any pupil creating a disturbance will be instantly evicted!' he shouted. And I started to twist my hair again. I couldn't stop doing it, those days. With the hair twisting I always fell into the dream of hiding in Milly-Molly-Mandy's cottage.

The projectionist started the film as if he was about to sit a hard exam. In a confusion of movement we saw men with guns and piupius running and crouching and firing little puffs of silent white smoke. A god's voice boomed, 'Rewi's forces decide to defy the enemy to the end.' More men ran. More little smoke-puffs hung in the air. I slumped down in my seat, two fingers twisting the lock of hair they always twisted, and tried to build the walls of my cottage around me. But all I saw was the smoke of the fire rising thinly beside the school road, and the drummer boy's hand rising and falling in its battle tuck.

Catcalling and whistling and stamping broke out at the back. The lights flashed on.

'I am *beside* myself!' cried Miss Audrey Littlewood, torch darting distractedly.

'*You, sir* – and you, sir – and *you*, sir,' roared the Headmaster, 'leave this theatre immediately! Proceed back at the double and wait for me in my office.' Veins stood out on his neck as he strode back down the aisle.

Standing at the back was a square quiet man, middle-aged. His arms were folded and he looked at no one.

'Proceed, proceed, Mr Turnbull,' shouted the Headmaster, arms flailing like a windmill at the projectionist's little window. The square quiet man rearranged his arms and looked at the floor.

The lights went off, the picture groaned into life. Soldiers in little pillbox hats ran and knelt and pointed guns like sticks. Puffs of smoke sprang over the rough ground. Maori warriors crouched in

The Bear from the North

fern. Rewi of Maniopoto bowed his head over his Great Earth and wept, and I put my head in my hands and wept for Miss Martin and Rewi of Maniopoto.

In the brilliant light outside we stumbled back to school. On the post office steps a group of river Maoris watched us go by. They were dressed in black and smoked tailor-mades, narrowing their eyes in the wind. The square quiet man walked at the back, not keeping in step, but watching everything there was to see.

At school, hair tousled by the wind, we stood in our ranks in the playground, waiting to be told what to do next. Beside the Headmaster stood the square quiet man. He looked at us once, and then looked at the trees by the fence.

'You will no doubt understand,' shouted the Headmaster, 'that we must all make way at the end of our work for new blood. Next week, you are to have a new Headmaster, Mr Preston.'

Pre-ston. A kind, quiet name.

The Headmaster looked at Mr Preston. 'Now, sir,' he said, 'you will wish to address your new pupils.'

Mr Preston drifted forward. He spoke into the wind so casually that we had to strain our ears.

'Maori haka?' he said. He gestured at the boys. No one moved. 'Come on – come on – give it a go,' he said. He directed the boys into a long line curving around the tennis court. Then he waved a finger at us girls. 'Come on, little warriors,' he said. We stood to attention. He twiddled his fingers at us and groaned. 'Relax,' he said, 'you'll make me tired out!'

He grinned. Then his arm shot up, his body fell into a long line, his hands rippled stiffly, and he stamped one foot.

'Ka mate! Ka mate!' he yelled.

We stood stock still. 'Who is Rewi of Maniopoto?' he shouted. 'Who will stand with him and do his haka? *I* move – *you* move – get into the rhythm!'

'Ka mate! Ka mate!' we piped.

'Make the Plains shake!' shouted Mr Preston.

We made the Plains shake. And when it was over and we were talking and laughing and calling out to Mr Preston to do it again, I looked over at the Headmaster. He stood to attention by his classroom steps, very grey, very thin, very tired. And his face was the face of the young frightened pupil-teacher in the photograph in the classroom, who had shouted all his life to control the big boys, to control the tree stumps, to keep one jump ahead with the slow painful reading of his books until dawn, in the long cruel winter nights of the Plains.

The Cousin from Holstein

Where did we come from?
From South Jutland in Denmark.
Why did we come?
To escape the German occupation after our defeat in the Slesvig-Holstein War. We came in a ship with sails like swans' wings, and when we got to New Zealand we locked and bolted the doors behind us.

But South Jutland got in. It followed us. One moment the land was New Zealand; kahikatea standing in the paddocks, supple-jack in the little patches of secret bush. Raffia baskets made by our clumsy fingers for Miss Martin. Lead farm animals for prizes in the Cadbury Cocoa tins, and Milly-Molly-Mandy going blackberrying on the Common. But on our mantelpiece South Jutland lived. It lived in a little wine-red wreath of wiry stems and berries, tytte-berries from the Jutland moors. In the autumn, said my Bedstemoder, our people boiled those tytte-berries into red soup and drank it. To keep away the sickness that the deep winter snow brought. And something else. They took in with that drink a part of the land into their blood, and they became part of their Great Earth. And it never let them go.

In the autumn in South Jutland, said my Bedstemoder, the land was covered with blue mist as the frost-moon rose. Through that mist the autumn trees burned their yellow fires, their red fires. In the autumn twilights of the Manawatu, my Bedstemoder watched her new land. And I saw that frost-moon rise, I saw the bare willow trees along the Foxton Line burn their yellow fires.

The Cousin from Holstein

Over the tytte-berry wreath hung a sad painting. Large black letters underneath said 'Retreat from the Dannevirke'. In it soldiers in long blue greatcoats and black snow-boots dragged a gun-carriage through deep snow. A tall soldier carrying a musket marched in front. His eyes were fixed on the frozen horizon. I knew his eyes. It was my Grandonkel Flemming. I told nobody of my discovery. I asked Grandonkel Flemming in the painting questions.

'What was it like?' I asked.

'Snowing,' he said, 'and the land frozen hard. We tried to hold our ancient ramparts, but the enemy poured over them. We retreated through the snow, carrying our wounded.'

Behind his head I saw the frozen fields stretching to the frontier; I heard the long sullen mutter of guns.

My Bedstemoder wore a dress with a high collar. Fastening the collar was an old Slesvig horned brooch made of ivory, garlanded with tiny silver wreaths of oak leaves. Her collar was shaped like a hussar's collar. I could see her, a young Jutland girl-warrior, dying silently in the snow for her Fatherland.

'Why did we come to New Zealand?' I asked.

Her nostrils flared like a brave war-horse.

'To get away from the Proos-i-ans!' she cried.

'Who are the Proos-i-ans?' I asked.

'Wicked men who took our Homeland!' she cried.

I think I saw a Proos-i-an only once, and it was such a muddle that I am not sure. It was Major Gore, come calling on his horse. Major Gore had *been* a warrior, that is why he rode his horse up people's drives, and yelled out his messages from on high, instead of getting down and knocking on people's doors, as a good Christian man *should* snapped my Bedstemoder.

One morning he walked his horse up my Bedstemoder's drive and yelled his message.

'I say — Mrs Westigad — ma - am?' he yelled, really quite gently. My Moder was doing little bits of useful visitor's work in my Bedstemoder's kitchen. She was no use at all with Major Gore. Every time she heard his voice from his horse she put her face into her hands and giggled. It was that old horse, she tried to explain,

The Bear from the North

and Major Gore's leggings and his fluting voice.

'I say – Mrs Westigid?' he called again. I rushed into the sitting room. My Bedstemoder was standing like a pillar of frost in the exact middle of her carpet.

'Proos-i-ans,' she hissed, 'sit on their horses outside the people's houses in South Jutland and shout. They do not knock at doors like true Christians.' Only she did not say those words in English. When they rode on to her land she forgot her English and became an old Danish dronning.

I peeped out of the window.

'Hey, little girl,' Major Gore yelled, grinning like one of his friendly dogs, 'is your granny at home?'

'Granny!' said my Bedstemoder in her grey-wolf voice. 'I am not *granny*!'

'Just thought I'd let you know,' shouted Major Gore, as friendly as could be, 'that one of your heifers wandered down the road. Ha ha! Been in my maize patch all morning. Ha ha! One of my chaps is bringin' it back now.'

My Bedstemoder advanced to the window. Major Gore anxiously cocked his good ear towards her.

'Thank you,' said my Bedstemoder. 'Your fences are a disgrace, therefore my poor old heifer goes into your maize patch. In future knock at my door!' But not in English she spoke. Nej. She spoke in her dronning Danish. The Danish of a frost-dronning.

We were saved by dear Far. He strolled up, and slapped Major Gore's old horse on its rump.

'Good heavens!' he said. 'That stupid old heifer again? I will come down in a tick and see to your fence!'

I peeped over my shoulder at my Bedstemoder. Who was the Proos-i-an?

'Your Bedstemoder,' said my kusine Maren in 1946, setting her plump capable hands in her lap, 'came from the *south* of Jutland.'

'The south?'

'They are different there,' said Kusine Maren 'from the northern Danes. They speak with a much more guttural accent. Incisive. A different pronunciation of Danish. Rather like the Germans.'

We were looking at the photographs. Every time a relation

The Cousin from Holstein

came, we looked at the photographs. My Fader was holding a great crowded one, mounted on serious-looking grey cardboard. He peered at it dreamily.

'Ah – here we have the Feast of Slesvig's Liberation,' he said. I peered over his shoulder. Hundreds of people were sitting at tables. Over their heads hung a forest of banners. At one side stood an army of grave girls. Over each grave girl's shoulder ran a beautiful sash.

'Dannebrog colours,' said Kusine Maren. 'Scarlet and white. Oh, we were busy that day! But we managed. Morning tea, hot dinner, afternoon tea and a little snack before home time!'

'Look,' said my Fader, 'there is all of us!' And there they were. Sitting right under the banners of Slesvig with the lions with coronets about their necks. Boys with cropped heads and long slanting eyes sat seriously behind vases of flowers. In the middle sat my Fader. He was the only one who was grinning.

'Ah, that was a great day!' he cried. 'In 1920 we won back our land. The King – old Christian the Tenth, he rode his big horse over the frontier. . . .

'Do not forget the child in white!' cried Kusine Maren.

'Aw,' said Far, 'that old king was always a good-natured man. He saw a little girl in white, holding up flowers to him. And he hoisted her up to give her legs a rest. Probably been hanging around that frontier all day, holding on to those flowers.'

'The King,' cried Maren with deep feeling, 'rode his horse through the frontier with the Danish child in white carrying her flowers. The people wept and cheered . . .' Her voice broke. My Fader came to the rescue.

'*All* day,' he said, 'we boys carted those big ferns in from the bush to make all fresh and green. Into the Palmerston North Show Buildings they went for the Feast of Slesvig's Liberation.'

I glanced at my cousin Erling, seventeen years old and from South Jutland. He had come from Denmark to see us, at the end of the Second World War. He had dark-gold hair, the colour of grass when the sun has burned it all summer long. The photographs had interrupted his telling me of the history of the War. He jerked his head at me. We went outside, into the chill autumn afternoon. A train hooted its long mournful sound on the way past the farm to

Wellington. I kicked a stone.

'Did you ever see a Proos-i-an?' I asked.

He laughed.

'A German,' he said. There was a short silence.

'In the occupation,' he said, 'we had to keep up our farm production. In the last stages, I used to take milk on a cart a long way down to the Co-operative before school. And that winter I was fifteen, there was deep snow. One morning there were drifts and I hauled and hauled but I couldn't get that cart to move. Then suddenly, it moved. I looked behind, and there was a German soldier. A Hitler boy. He was my age. Coat around his old boots, cap too big for him, down over his eyes. He had a great big useless old-fashioned rifle flopping over his shoulder. And he was pushing my cart. My God, how he pushed. We went all the way down that road, squeaking over the snow. And all the time he droned on, 'Good morning, I am your cousin from Holstein. Good morning, I too push a milk-cart at home. I know the knack of pushing milk-carts. Good morning, I am hungry, I am your cousin from Holstein. I am hungry, I am your cousin from Holstein. Speak to me, cousin . . .'

'You understood his German?' I asked. Erling looked glumly at his feet.

'He spoke in Danish,' he said. 'There's always been a mixup on that frontier. Danes on both sides, Danish spoken on both sides. Marrying each other.'

'Was he your cousin, Erling?'

'Ja,' said Erling. 'He had gone to our farmhouse. They shut the door on him. He was in the German army.'

'Erling!' I shouted, clutching at his sleeve. 'He was only a boy, he was starving! Did you give him some milk? Erling?'

'I didn't say a word to him,' said Erling. 'We didn't speak to Germans.' He walked slowly back to the house.

I went over to the gate and hung on to it, gazing savagely at the pine wind breaks raking the red sunset sky. In the high toppling clouds I saw Grandonkel Flemming hauling the gun-carriage. I saw King Christian the Tenth riding with the child in white over the frontier. Then I looked down at my feet at the mud and stones of our drive. And burning in my eyes I saw the cousin from Holstein, pushing that squeaking milk-cart over the deep snow of 1945. You see such things for the rest of your life.

The Growing of Astrid Westergaard

One day my Fader said, 'On that waste land at the back of the potato garden I am going to make a fine canal for ducks.'

'*Ducks*, Astrid,' said my Moder. 'White as fine porcelain. They followed me so sweetly on their yellow feet when I was a girl on our farm.'

'*Ducks*,' I said, and I saw myself as a duck-girl, in the national costume of our district in South Jutland, talking to our ducks in the old language that only ducks know. I would become famous throughout the Manawatu as Astrid, the wise duck-woman.

'Now,' said Far in the voice of a great and wise leader, 'who are going to be my strong workmen?'

'Who is there but us, blessed fool?' asked my Moder tenderly.

My Fader waved an arm at the horizon.

'Forward!' he cried.

We marched out behind him, kerchiefs knotted strongly behind our ears.

'Beneath this land,' cried Far, tearing enthusiastically at the long grass, 'we might find kings' hoards. If it was Jutland,' he added hastily.

My Mor straightened her back and looked at the distant sky. 'In Jutland once,' she said, 'my Fader when ploughing uncovered a hoard.'

'Karen,' said my Fader. 'Now you never told me that.'

'It was a silver broadsword and a ring, just under the ground,' said my Moder. 'My Onkel Johannes rode to the village and told the people and everyone came out to our farm, some in carts, some on horseback, and some running.'

'A piece of our glorious past,' cried Far, 'for all to clap eyes on again!'

'They got the news to Copenhagen just as fast as they could and a man came from the museum there with wings on his feet.'

'And all would come from far and near to see our history,' said my Fader nostalgically.

'All came from far and near,' said Mor.

'Far . . .' I said faintly, 'do you think . . .?'

'Nej, nej, nej,' cried Fader, 'not here, not here! But, ah, what a proud day that would have been for your village.'

'A proud day it was,' said my Moder.

And, thoughtfully, we bent to our grass-pulling again.

We gave Morning Talks once a week, taking turns from a list with a splendid name, a Roster. Mr Preston sat on top of a desk at the back of the room and plugged away at lengthening our talks and improving our vocabulary. He nagged at 'the Gangsters', who tended to wither away when facing the class alone and unaided. The Gangsters always gave the same talks – they made me so hungry!

'Las' noight,' mumbled the Gangsters, 'We played round a bit 'n Billy fell 'n the crik 'n Mum sung out tea's ready . . .'

'Good, good,' shouted Mr Preston, 'now tell us what you had for tea.'

The Gangsters always rolled their eyes like wild steers at that point. Then they looked primly out of the windows.

'Meat 'n p'tatas 'n cabbage,' they said in a baby's whisper and closed their lips grimly. It was indecent, said their stony faces, to pester and pester a bloke about the secrets of his home.

'Come on, come on, old man!' Mr preston would cheerfully cry. 'You must have had some pudding. Go on – make us feel *hungry*!' The Gangsters looked at their feet then, and sulked. Then they came clean, as real gangsters were always doing down at the Regal Picture Theatre in the Saturday matinées.

'Jelly 'n fruit 'n stuff,' they muttered.

'Fine, fine!' shouted Mr Preston. 'Lots of vitamins in fruit, class. Lots of growing material! You'll be giants in a flash and touch this ceiling if you eat lots of fruit and vegetables.'

We all looked at the ceiling. Giants! Oh, it was rich! We roared with laughter, on and on. He gave us jokes like that all day. Especially jokes about rabbits. Carrots, he told us, made you see in the dark.

'Hands up,' shouted Mr Preston, 'all those people who have seen a rabbit wearing glasses!'

Out of the silence came my deep bellowing Jutland laugh. And Mr Preston said, 'Well, Astrid, when I'm an old, old man, and nobody laughs at my jokes any more. I'll close my eyes and remember your laugh. And that'll cheer me up.'

He said that – he said *that*! And I just laughed without covering my mouth, for ever more.

That morning it was my Morning Talk. I was first on the Roster.

'Good morning, boys and girls,' I said. (We started like that.) 'My Fader is building us a fine canal for ducks to live in. I am to look after them too and learn the cry that makes ducks run to you. And my Moder says that if you are lucky, in Jutland the plough may uncover ancient hoards of the old Jutland kings. Her Fader one day uncovered a ring and a sword! Any questions, class?' (We ended like that.)

Cherry's hand waved.

'Yes, Cherry Taylor?' I asked. (Mr Preston said that we were undergoing a training in the processes of democratic government, so we used *whole* names, just as if we didn't know our best friends inside out.)

'Do you think your father will uncover treasure in your duck canal, Astrid?' asked Cherry in a detached, official voice.

'He says not in this country, Cherry,' I said, crisp as crisp. Then I pressed my lips efficiently together and sat down.

'Now,' said Mr Preston, 'that raises an interesting point. In European countries – for example Jutland in Denmark where Astrid's people come from – people sometimes dig up real treasure. And in England . . .'

You see? He said 'Jutland in Denmark where Astrid's people come from', just as easily as anyone could say 'the Manawatu in New Zealand'. Just as easily as that!

The Growing of Astrid Westergaard

After school I biked home as fast as a bog-witch in case Fader had finished the canal and the ducks were already swimming restlessly around waiting for me to give them their dinner. Far and Mor, dirt-stained, hair in spikes from the wind, were drinking their afternoon coffee. *Something was in the air.*

'Have you finished the canal?' I cried.

'The canal?' said Far. 'Oh – no.' He drank some coffee. 'I can't believe it,' he said to Mor. 'After what we said – it's like a sign.'

'Do you think we are imagining it?' asked my Moder in a worried voice.

'Nej, nej, nej. They were at all stages, all stages. I tell you, they've found heaps of those thing in the district, all the time.'

'But *here*,' said my Moder, 'in our garden.'

'What is in our garden?' I shouted. 'Silver swords?'

'Nej,' said my Moder. She looked excited and swallowed her coffee quickly.

'Secrets,' said Far.

'You had better wear your pleated skirt to school tomorrow, Astrid,' said Mor.

'No work for you in the waste land tonight, Astrid,' said Fader. 'It's much too muddy.'

'Ducks,' I said deeply and happily, 'will love that!'

'Class,' said Mr Preston the next morning, 'attention!'

We sat up and put our hands fiercely on our heads.

'No, no, no, not that *again*,' moaned Mr Preston, sagging at the knees. 'Not that Devil's Island stunt again.'

'Haw, haw, haw!' roared the Gangsters at their kind of joke.

'Now,' said Mr Preston, 'we are going on an expedition to a secret destination, and at the end we're going to find treasure.'

'Silver swords!' bawled a Gangster. I went as pink as a poppy.

'No further clues,' said Mr Preston. 'Last one at the gate is a duck's egg!' A *duck's egg*.

We marched, with no drummer boy from the Napoleonic Wars, steadily up Number One Line.

'Mr Preston, Sir,' I ventured, 'we're getting awfully close to our house. *Awfully* close.'

'You don't say,' drawled Mr Preston, like Humphrey Bogart in

The Bear from the North

his trench coat and the hat tilted glamorously over one eye.

We walked some more. I couldn't bear it any longer.

'Mr Preston, Sir,' I said diffidently, 'I can see my Moder's washing from here. We're getting frightfully close, *frightfully close*.' Then an amazing thing happened. Mr Preston led us straight up our drive and through our gate!

'Girls and boys,' I gabbled, 'this is my house, and there's my window and there's Bor the dog's kennel and . . .'

Nobody answered, they were so surprised.

We marched over the lawn and over the bridge and past the vegetable garden and through the hedge and into our waste land. And there was my Fader standing to attention holding his bright clean spade and wearing his flannel trousers and his cricket blazer. And there were Mor and Tante Helga and Bedstemoder. Tante Helga was wearing her longish dirndl with the flower embroidered straps and blouse and my Bedstemoder was standing very tall indeed in her good black with her best Jutland silver jewellery – the large silver jewellery from olden times. Then I saw why she was standing so straight. Opposite her stood an old, old Maori man and woman. The old man had on his good suit and a watch chain with a sort of greenstone tooth hanging from it, and the old woman was dressed in *her* good black and she had on all her jewellery too – gold and greenstone and long greenstone ear-rings under her fashionable tea-cosy hat. She and my Bedstemoder looked at each other with gleaming eyes and each tried to stand taller than the other.

'People, stand and listen,' said Mr Preston, showing us off. He walked over to my Fader, and there on the ground by my Fader's feet were neat piles of stones – some plain, some scratched, some chipped, and some in a faint chisel shape. But rough – not polished. They were the same stones as the ones in the creek. No silver rings. No shining broad swords.

'Fader!' I cried in a voice like weeping. He had gone mad and thought he had discovered a king's hoard like the Jutland ones. My Moder shook her head slightly at me, then she leaned back and admired me in my class. Her eyes were brilliant with happiness.

'Say good morning, class,' said Mr Preston.

'Good-morn-ing!' we roared sheepishly.

'Godmorgen,' said my Moder and Fader and Bedstemoder and Tante Helga.

Then my Bedstemoder said in her dronning voice, 'Velkommen!'

'That, class,' said Mr Preston, 'is a Danish greeting of welcome. Remember the words – widen your vocabulary.'

My heart burst with pride. He went slowly over to the two old Maoris and said something in *real Maori*. Thunderstruck, we watched him rub noses!

Then my Fader stooped and picked up one of the carefully washed stones.

'Children,' he said, and his voice shook. I clenched my fists. 'Hundreds of years ago some Maori people lived in this garden. They fished for eels in the creek and cooked them on their fires – here. And when they had time, they sat on this very ground and made adzes – tools – out of the creek stones.'

'Adzes – tools – new language,' Mr Preston warned us. He addressed Far as if he was at a meeting. 'Your daughter Astrid told us that in Denmark your people have uncovered discoveries from the past.'

Far's face worked with pride.

'In Jutland,' he said, 'kings' hoards have been uncovered on our farms.' Then his voice became strong. 'No silver swords, no crown here, but treasure of a different kind. The roots, the history of our country. Here our long-ago brothers sat down by their fires and made tools.'

The two old Maoris slowly moved over to the stones, raised their faces to the sky, and started to chant; a chant with only one note in it, and sometimes a cry, a falling-away at the end of a breath. They were talking to the stones, and to some people in the earth and the sky as strong as Odin, as strong as Freya. And to God who made us all.

But the chant was the sound of the stones and the creek bed and the bush at its edge and the dust and the grass and the wind of the Plains.

And I bowed my head and began my long life's journey, the learning by heart of the stones and the grass and the wind of our new homeland. And at last I would call each man my Fader, each woman my Moder, each girl my sister, and each boy my brother. In *our* country.

The growing of Astrid Westergaard began.

Farvel

You know, all today they have been here. In my house. A door opens by itself. A hand raps on the window glass like the crack of winter ice breaking up in the old country. A hand touches my shoulder and I turn ready to hear somebody say,

'Use the new jam for lunch. It has set so *nice!*' There is nobody there.

Somebody touches my hair, absent-mindedly, as they used to, gazing out of the windows, looking at the sky, at the land. Our land. It speaks, you know. Or a voice sings. Suddenly. And you must listen, every sense alert.

Who touched my hair?

The door shut with no wind to do that.

The house is full of them. I hear tag-ends of words, laughter. Then a wind pounces on the garden, the trees. Grass, leaves, shiver, ripple with silver, with laughter, with calling voices.

'Hoy!' I call to them in Danish, 'you come now to your nice lunch!' As if they *need* lunch, those ones. They have no desire for this world's food any more. They are with God now.

Then I hear that one living voice from a month ago. Calling from her farmhouse drive, with its trees leaning from a lifetime of the north-westerlies. She as bent as her trees, out on the Tainui Line.

'Farvel, mit eget kaere barn!'

'Farewell, my own darling child!'

I turn in the road. I know that cry. I call, with a laugh, you know?

'Nej – nej. You are not saying farewell to me for ever. No death for you yet!'

But she is not laughing. Again comes that cry, bleak as the wind –

'Farvel, mit eget kaere barn!'

And then she looks at my face. She is learning it all over again. She is leaving us. Soon. She will know the time. She is warning me.

'Nej!' I call. 'Not yet.'

I look at her face, not just her face, but all the faces that one by one have gone. I see her stand out in the road, watching me as if she can never have enough of looking. Not just my face, all our faces. We look the same, you see. So I do my part. I wave, I shout.

'Farvel! Tante Helga Westergaard, you are *great*!'

She knows. She breaks into a broad smile and waves. I go, but the figure left behind on that road never moves, never blinks its sea-pale eyes from fear that they miss one last, small glance.

She is being drawn back into that other country. From the first breath I took, I heard its music; the men and women singing. Remembering too, you understand, the thin soil, the howling winter weather. But, being so young, I only thought of that great multitude of our left-behind people, their faces shining with love, singing in a world filled with light. And that was Europe to me. That was my Denmark. There were the singers, and the sacred dancers, moving rank on slow rank. And now they come to claim her, those dancers, and she goes to meet them, her hands outflung in greeting, so tall, walking so softly.

The wind still blows.

'Ah,' I say to the voices in the rooms, to the laughter in the trees, in the sky, 'you be quiet now. I have to think. I have to be with her.'

Our language was spoken in a rapid, cold stream, like the water rushing in its courses over the moors, and gleaming so still in the marshes where we lived in Jutland. I was always part of a group, a frieze of women, very tall, in the long grass of a paddock, or looking out of a window. Always standing, once or twice in the busy day, one hand on the hip, the other used to help the meaning along – coming delicately down to rest on certain words that mattered. They talked as they danced, the movements spare and

Farvel

ceremonial, leaving things to be understood. Taking in, breathing in, the messages of the land and sky of the Manawatu. I learned the spoken words, and with my skin, my eyes, my senses, endlessly took in the signs, the changing light of sun and colour and water, the line of hills and plains, the movement of birds. The signs were the magic signs learned by our people long ago in Denmark. They had the power, my Bedstemoder said, to see them, to use them in the new lands. They knew the secrets of food-growing, the places to find water, how to build shelter, and the patterns of the seasons. We learned all that so that our bodies and our spirits could grow, side by side. And they had the power to change themselves into the shapes of birds – the swan, the wild geese, the eagle, the falcon.

The first people here, said my Bedstemoder, had the same powers. Here it was that the sea birds and the ghost-herons became the souls of the people who had died. Who journeyed back to their home, to the sun at their death, as we do.

When I first saw those people, the Maoris, at the Recreation Ground in a huge gathering, long ago, I knew she spoke the truth. There they *were*, standing under the soft thunder of the macrocarpas. They wore the long mantles, and the birds' feathers sweeping back in their hair; half men, half birds. As certain men and women in Denmark changed into swans, eagles, so did they. So I always saw that race and ours, able to read the signs, to haunt the sky on wings, an irresistible sweep of wings; sky-walkers.

Tante Helga is loosening the cord. Coming into my ears is a voice.
'My child, I need Thee.'

So I go and put on a more suitable dress and wash my face, making myself neat for Tante Helga. I brush my hair in front of the mirror, not looking into it, and then I do. I see the face of an aging woman; the lines, the bones of my people. They have stamped me with their image for ever. But also on it, the squint-lines of our summers here; the ridges and hollows left by the sun and dust of the new country, *my* country.

I go to the veranda and lean over. The sun beats down. The river is shrunken, its black banks glitter with mica that my Bedstemoder said was treasure, dragonfire, here as in Denmark.

Then, like a sigh, up the drying river bed flies a heron, that one that lives on the little island. A grey heron, but today changed in the flat light to black paper, a soul, starting its journey to the sea. That is my sign. So I walk out into the beating sun, to the fence that borders the paddock, that reaches to the river.

I stand and look at the land. The ghost-heron has vanished. And I *cannot* stop my grief, my tears that turn down my wind-furrowed face. I look at our land, and the river, and I cannot make sense of it, or hear Tante Helga's voice. All I can remember are her cheek bones, the blue northern eyes of our lost people. I weep like a little child. Out of my shameful gaping mouth I call.

'Tante Helga. Tante! We are lost for ever.'

And her voice comes, deep in my ear, loosening the cord, but still gossiping on, as she did, one summer afternoon, on the lawn behind me.

'There your Bedstemoder, Abild Westergaard, lay on the second day of her death, in her room, in this house. And your Moder and I peeped out of the kitchen window into the farmyard and saw the Maoris, and she said, "Helga, they are here."'

'And they were. Some sitting, some standing, and the Chief standing looking out over the land. They were quite still; warfalcons at rest.

'Your Mother gripped my hand, so *tight*.

'"They are from the Pa," she whispered, "where Mor went. She loved them all. Come now."

'I stood in front of the Chief, the one with the long feather sweeping back from his head. We looked at each other. I greeted him in Danish, he greeted me in Maori. Then we turned and stood with his people, our neighbours. We touched their faces, in their way of greeting, and we stood here. Our hair blew about, but we stood so still with them, helping Abild Westergaard begin her journey to sun-fire. It was a great honour they did us that day.'

The old lilting voice dies away to a murmur, to silence, in my mind.

Who are left now? They and us, changed a little, but still knowing who we are. Using our old knowledge, and our new.

I look over the paddocks at my neighbour, Rangi Katene. Her house looks at me through the trees. I often stand in them in their circle of ancient trunks, and the wind hisses through their leaves

Farvel

and combs the grass at my feet. Sacred trees. Their roots reach down to underground rivers, dragon-lairs. The house and Rangi know those messages from the dark.

And now, you know something strange? The wind has dropped. There is a golden light, that light when the sun is spent, when the dust motes turn to golden bees in the air. Every grass blade in the parched earth you can see, golden wires. The head-dresses those ancient dancers wore in the Jutland festival, they were made like wheat-ears, red-gold, quivering over their still faces. Faces that knew everything. Like my Tante Helga. Somehow, the power of the Old Religion slipped into the New Religion in Jutland. God and the Old Magic mixed together. I have worked out that truth, by myself.

The golden bees of the sun swarm over the paddocks. It seems to me not a trick of light, but a gift from God that I see those Maoris and Danes and English, now clear, now blurred, standing facing their lands. My house, like Rangi's, reaches its roots down to the heart of this land. Our roots are the same. We have our people, living and dead, around us for ever.

Canoe, Viking ship, foam-necked, set out together on the last journey north, over the sea-roads to world's end.

So I let go of the fence post I am gripping, scrub my face dry with a knuckled fist, and lift my eyes to be blinded by the light that welcomes Helga Westergaard at the end of her journey.

Oh, my brothers and sisters, see how our hands join together as we farewell our great Dead.

Farvel. Farvel.